Deep Blend

'Where singles sip, seduce and surrender.'

By Simon S. Steel

Deep Blend

Copyright © 2025 by Simon S. Steel

Dedications:

For Amira – Because Queens are never crowned alone.

Acknowledgements:

I owe gratitude to those who helped shape this book —
the readers who inspired Victorias story, the quiet cafés
that gave me refuge, and to every friend who reminded
me that imagination is always worth following.

Prologue

Not everyone finds the door.

It isn't marked. It isn't advertised. You don't stumble upon it by chance on your way to the office or between errands. No — Deep Blend is only for those who are invited, and those who are ready.

When I first stepped inside, I thought it was just a café. A quiet refuge for people like me — single, busy, tired of the noise and the clatter of the world. Leather chairs, dark wood, bookshelves, silence. A place to breathe.

But Deep Blend was never just a café.

It was a sanctuary. A stage. A kingdom.

I learned quickly that within those walls, singles didn't just sip coffee. They played. They performed. They surrendered. And I discovered something I'd never dared admit to myself before: I loved being watched. I loved controlling who broke, who begged, who came undone.

That was the beginning.

What came next… was Ecosexation.

Chapter 1
The Door

I paused in front of the black door, the one without a sign. To anyone else, it could have been an electricity substation or a storage unit. For me, today, it was either going to be a sanctuary or the most embarrassing mistake I'd made since trying a juice cleanse that ended with me eating three pork pies and a block of cheddar at midnight.

I smoothed down my coat, checked my lipstick in my phone screen, and pressed the brass buzzer.

The door opened two inches. A woman in black stood there, slim, elegant, holding a tablet like she was checking in guests at a secret embassy. Her eyes were calm, watchful.

"Membership ID?" she asked.

I reached into my bag and pulled out the piece of paper. "007," I said. "Though I left my Aston Martin at home."

The woman's mouth twitched. "Victoria Jennings?"

"Unless you're about to tell me I'm dead and this is the afterlife."

That earned a smile. The woman stepped back, opening the door fully. "I'm Amira. Welcome to Deep Blend."

The street noise disappeared behind me as I stepped inside. It was like crossing into another century. Thick curtains muffled the world outside. The air smelled of roasted coffee and beeswax polish.

Dark wood panelling stretched along the walls, interrupted by bookshelves stacked with hardbacks in neat rows. Leather armchairs and sofas were arranged in conversational clusters, softened by potted plants and low brass lamps that glowed amber.

There was no clatter of crockery, no hiss of steam, no barista shouting "VICTY?" as though names were optional. Just the low hum of the coffee machine, the faint rustle of pages, and a stillness that made my shoulders drop.

For the first time in months, I breathed properly.

Amira walked with me, quiet but present, pointing things out like a museum guide. "Coffee is self-serve. Freshly ground, always stocked. Snacks are in the cabinets—cards only, no cash. Each table has a dial: red for privacy, green if you're open to conversation. No one will disturb you unless you invite it. We keep it that way."

"And what if someone ignores the dial?" I asked, eyebrow raised.

"Then you let me know." Amira tapped her pin. "I deal with it."

I liked that. Efficient. Firm. Very… club-like. I wasn't sure whether to bow or salute.

There were maybe a dozen people inside. A man in a linen jacket reading The Times. A young woman with discreet headphones tapping at her laptop. A pair of women on opposite sides of the room, each with a book propped against a teacup, utterly content in silence.

No one looked up. No one cared. I could have stripped naked and sung 'I Will Survive', and they'd probably just sigh and adjust their bookmarks.

I poured myself a coffee, rich and black, and carried it to a leather chair by the far corner. A brass dial gleamed on the table beside her. I turned it firmly to red, sat down, and opened my book — the same book I'd been failing to get through for six months.

Outside, buses sighed and couples bickered over umbrellas. Inside, there was only the warmth of the lamp and the weight of a good chair.

I took my first sip, closed my eyes, and thought: 'This. This I could get used to.'

Then I noticed the man in the linen jacket glancing at me over the rim of his paper. I caught his eye by accident. He smiled.

I muttered into my coffee cup: "Oh bloody hell, not already."

✦ ✦ ✦

Chapter 2

The Quiet Chair

I settled deeper into the leather chair, my coffee warming my hands, the amber lamp at my shoulder throwing a golden pool across the page of my book. The page I had read three times already, and still couldn't recall. Not because the words weren't worth remembering, but because my own kept getting in the way.

Fifty-two. A successful businesswoman, owner of Jennings & Co, consultancy to half the firms in the City. On paper, my life ticked every box. Financially secure. A house in Hampstead. A wardrobe that could pass as armor in any boardroom.

And single. The word people said like it was a diagnosis.

I sipped my coffee and smirked. At least here, there were no sympathetic tilts of the head, no well-meaning friends whispering "I just don't understand how you're still single" as though I were a puzzle missing a corner piece.

No. Deep Blend had rules. No judgement. No intrusion. No need for explanations.

I let my gaze wander around the room. The man in linen still rustled his paper. The young woman with headphones typed furiously, pausing now and again to chew her pen like she wanted to kill it. A middle-aged man by the fireplace was asleep, head tilted back, snoring softly. And nobody cared.

I loved that.

It hadn't always been like this. I thought back to my last "ordinary café experience" three months earlier, on the high street near my office. I'd gone in needing ten minutes' peace, and instead:

- A barista shrieking "OAT MILK FLAT WHITE FOR VICTY?" every twenty seconds.

- A toddler launching rice cakes like confetti.

- A man with a laptop taking a loud Zoom call about "synergy" while everyone tried not to stab him with a teaspoon.

By the time I left, I was covered in oat crumbs and had only managed to answer two emails, one of which autocorrected "client proposal" to "silent disposal." Not a good look.

And then there was dating. God help me.

I chuckled into my coffee, remembering my last attempt. A blind date set up by a friend of a friend — because apparently being single in your fifties meant you had no say in your own arrangements.

His name was Martin. He arrived late, sweating, carrying a shopping bag that appeared to contain three tins of baked beans.

"Sorry," he said, breathless, as though they were mid-marathon. "Tesco was doing a deal."

The evening went downhill from there. He ordered Spaghetti Bolognese and spent the entire meal slurping it like a Hoover with a vendetta. He told me three times about his cholesterol, twice about his ex-wife's new car, and once about his bowel habits. When the bill came, he suggested splitting it "fifty-fifty" despite the fact I had eaten a side salad and drunk tap water.

I'd smiled sweetly, paid for my share, and left him with his beans.

That had been the moment I decided: no more. No more noisy cafés, no more sympathy dates, no more explanations. I was done.

And then, like some divine reward for putting my foot down, I stumbled across the article about Deep Blend.

I looked around again. The place was discreetly full, but peaceful. Nobody stared. Nobody shouted. I could sit here and simply be.

My eyes drifted to the brass dial on the table. Red, for privacy. Green, for conversation.

I smirked. The idea was ridiculous, and yet… genius. A built-in permission slip. How many times had I wanted that in life? At board meetings, on dates, at family gatherings. Dial red: don't even try me. Dial green: I'm listening.

I reached out, fingers brushing the dial, then pulled back. Not yet. Not today. Today was Mine.

Still, I could feel the man in the linen jacket glance my way again. Harmless, polite, but there.

I smiled into my coffee. 'Not yet, darling. You'll have to earn it.'

With that, I opened my book to the start of the chapter, and let the hush of Deep Blend wrap around me.

For the first time in years, Victoria Jennings wasn't performing. She wasn't explaining. She wasn't being defined by anyone else.

I was simply Victoria. And for now, that was more than enough.

Chapter 3
The First Green

The second time I walked into Deep Blend, I didn't hesitate at the door. I pressed the buzzer, announced "007" with enough Bond-girl flourish to make Amira raise an eyebrow, and strolled in as though I'd been coming for years.

I'd earned my chair. The wingback in the far corner, leather soft as butter, with a lamp that gave the perfect pool of light for reading. I headed straight for it, coffee in hand, dial firmly set to red.

Half an hour passed in blissful silence. I almost forgot I was surrounded by people — until the sound of a chair shifting caught my attention.

It was the man in linen. Same seat as last time, paper folded neatly, a small espresso in front of him. Today, though, the brass dial at his table had been turned to green.

I smirked. Bold.

I returned to my book.

Ten minutes later, a shadow fell across my page. "Excuse me," a voice said, polite, clipped. "Would you mind if I joined you?"

I looked up. Linen Jacket himself. Late fifties, I guessed. Distinguished, silver at the temples. Smelled faintly of cedarwood.

My eyes flicked to my own dial, still on red. I tapped it with one finger. "I'm afraid the system is quite clear, Mr…?"

He smiled faintly. "Carter. Daniel Carter."

"Mr Carter, then. Red means no entry. Rather like a stoplight. I'm sure you've seen one before."

His smile didn't falter. "Forgive me. I thought perhaps you were… flexible."

I snapped my book shut. "I am, Mr Carter. Just not here. Try the green table by the fireplace. The gentleman snoring will adore your company."

He chuckled softly, bowed — actually bowed — and withdrew.

When he'd gone, I reopened my book, though I wasn't reading. I could feel Amira's gaze from the corner of the room, approving, almost amused.

Later, when I rose to leave, Amira intercepted me at the door.

"Handled beautifully," she murmured. "Not everyone respects the system at first. But they learn."

I gave her a sly smile. "I've been teaching men to respect my stop signs for thirty years. This was just a refresher course."

Amira's laugh followed me out onto the street.

That evening, I sat at my kitchen table with a glass of Tempranillo and my shoes off, replaying the scene in my head.

Daniel Carter. Polished, confident, perfectly civil. The type of man who probably had an entire wardrobe of linen jackets and a golf membership somewhere in Surrey. The type who thought rules were advisory, not mandatory.

I found myself smiling, which annoyed me. "Oh for God's sake," I muttered aloud, "he broke café protocol. That should be a hanging offence."

And yet. He'd been disarming, I had to admit. That little bow had been absurdly charming, like something out of an old film. Which was exactly the problem. I didn't want Cary Grant. I wanted peace, coffee, and a chair that didn't squeak.

I topped up my glass, leaning back against the counter. Perhaps that was the danger of Deep Blend. The very absence of noise, chaos, and pressure made every interaction stand out in sharp relief. One man looking across the room felt like a declaration. One question felt like seduction.

"Red means red," I said firmly, raising my glass to the empty kitchen. "And I intend to keep it that way."

Still, when I went to bed, I wondered — not for the first time — what colour Daniel Carter's dial would be tomorrow.

Chapter 4
Turning the Tables

I arrived earlier than usual the next morning. I told myself it was because I had a client call nearby, but if I were honest, it was curiosity. I wanted to see if Daniel Carter would appear again, linen jacket and all.

And there he was. Same seat, same folded 'Times'. Only today his dial gleamed red.

I chuckled under I breath. Oh, perfect.

I poured my coffee, sauntered past his table, and caught the faintest flicker of his eyes above the page. He didn't move, didn't acknowledge me, but I was sure he'd seen me. He radiated that air of studied indifference men adopted when they desperately wanted to be noticed.

I sat at my own table for a while, dial on green, feigning interest in my book. Nothing. He didn't so much as twitch.

Cheeky sod.

I stood, carrying my cup, and approached his table. "Excuse me," I said sweetly. "Would you mind if I joined you?"

His paper lowered. His eyes met mine. Calm, grey, faintly amused. He tapped his dial. "I'm afraid the system is quite clear, Ms...?"

"Jennings. Victora Jennings."

"Ms Jennings. Red means no entry. Rather like a stoplight. I'm sure you've seen one before."

I laughed out loud, a proper, unrestrained laugh that turned a few heads. "Well played. That was mine, wasn't it?"

"Word for word," he said, folding his paper neatly. "Barrister. Retired. Memory is an occupational hazard."

I pulled out the chair opposite, ignoring the dial. "Then let me test that memory, Mr Carter. Do you remember what I said about rules?"

He raised an eyebrow. "That they're only worth breaking if they annoy the right person."

"Exactly." I leaned forward slightly, resting my chin on my hand, my eyes sparkling. "And I do believe you're the right person."

For the first time, his composure shifted. Just a flicker — amusement mixed with interest. He placed his paper aside and studied me properly.

"You don't strike me as someone who joins quiet cafés to follow rules."

"Oh, I do love rules," I said, twirling a strand of hair idly around my finger. "I just love bending them more."

"Dangerous habit."

"Occupational hazard." I tilted my head, letting my hair fall over one shoulder as I leaned in. The neckline of my blouse dipped ever so slightly, and I caught his eyes flicker downward before snapping back to her face.

"Caught you," I said softly, lips curving into a sly smile.

His mouth twitched. "Barristers don't get caught."

"You just did," I teased, sitting back and sipping my coffee. "And I didn't even need cross-examination."

The ice was broken now, the fencing replaced by a different kind of game. He asked what I did. I told him I ran my own consultancy, without apology. He raised an impressed eyebrow. I returned the favour when he revealed he had spent three decades at the Old Bailey.

"So you argue for a living," I said. "That explains everything."

"And you tell CEOs what to do," he countered. "So we're evenly matched."

I tilted my head again, feigning innocence. "Or a disaster waiting to happen."

"Or both," he said smoothly.

Eventually, I stood, chair scraping softly on the polished floor. "Well, Mr Carter, this has been… tolerable."

"High praise," he said, rising slightly from his chair in an old-fashioned gesture that made me secretly swoon.

I smirked, turning back toward my own table. "Don't get used to it."

Back at my chair, I flipped my dial firmly to red, picked up my book, and pretended to read while my pulse beat a little faster than usual.

That night, at home with a glass of Rioja, I caught myself smiling at the memory. I shouldn't have teased him. I certainly shouldn't have leaned in like that. But the look on his face — the flicker, the slip — had been utterly worth it.

"Oh, Vicky, you wicked cow," I muttered, topping up my glass.

I was supposed to have come to Deep Blend for peace. For quiet. For freedom.

And now here I was, sparring with a barrister and enjoying every minute.

✦ ✦ ✦

Chapter 5
The Rules of Engagement

For the third morning in a row, I arrived at Deep Blend earlier than usual. I hated myself for it. I had work to do, emails waiting, a proposal draft to send to a client who thought urgency was a lifestyle choice. And yet here I was, pausing outside the discreet black door like a schoolgirl hoping the handsome teacher was already in class.

He was.

Daniel Carter sat at his usual table, linen jacket crisp, newspaper folded with surgical precision. His dial gleamed green.

I strolled past him, deliberately setting my own to red. He didn't look up — not directly. But the corner of his mouth twitched.

Oh, he'd noticed.

I lasted twelve minutes before the silence broke my resolve. I flipped my dial to green with exaggerated ceremony and waited.

"Good morning, Ms Jennings," came the voice, smooth as velvet, from two tables away.

I didn't look up from my book. "Mr Carter. I see you've embraced traffic-light culture. Any plans to indicate before changing lanes?"

"Depends who's in the car with me," he replied.

I chuckled, finally meeting his eyes. "Careful. I'm a terrible passenger. Always grabbing the wheel."

"I've no doubt," he said, rising with his cup and strolling over to my table. He gestured politely at the empty chair.

I nodded. "Green does mean go, after all."

We began with small talk. Or what passed for it in our hands — weaponised observations, sharpened like blades and cushioned with smiles.

"So," I said, twirling a strand of hair. "A barrister. Retired. Does that mean you've shouted 'Objection!' in a real courtroom, or is that just American television nonsense?"

"I've shouted far worse," Daniel said. "Mostly at judges who fell asleep."

I laughed, leaning forward, chin in hand. "I like you already. Anyone who heckles authority is worth a second coffee."

He sipped his espresso, eyes not leaving mine. "And you? Consultancy, you said? You tell people how to run their businesses?"

"Correction," I said, raising a finger. "I tell men how to run their businesses while they pretend it was their idea. There's an art to it."

"Manipulation?" he suggested.

"Survival," I corrected, arching an eyebrow. "Besides, I prefer the term 'gentle guidance.' Sounds less threatening."

His eyes flickered down, just briefly, as I leaned a little further forward. My blouse slipped just enough to remind him I was not merely witty, but woman.

Caught. Again.

"Eyes up, Mr Carter," I murmured. "This is a conversation, not an optician's test."

He cleared his throat, smiling wryly. "You're dangerous."

"Darling, you've no idea."

By now, a few of the other members had begun to notice. Not openly — that would have been gauche. But the man by the fireplace lowered his paper an inch too long. The young woman with the headphones glanced up and smirked before returning to her typing.

And Amira… Amira had appeared in her quiet way, standing near the coffee machine, eyes flicking between me and Daniel with a look halfway between amusement and warning.

I leaned back, deliberately loud enough for Amira to hear. "Tell me, Mr Carter, how many traffic laws have you broken in your career?"

Daniel tilted his head. "Enough to know the fine is worth the thrill."

I laughed so loudly the room stirred. Amira's gaze sharpened.

"Careful," I whispered, lips curving into a smile. "We're attracting an audience."

"Then let's give them a performance," he said softly, lifting his cup to mine.

We clinked porcelain, silent and electric.

When I left that afternoon, Amira intercepted me at the door.

"You do realise," Amira said, voice low, "this isn't meant to be a stage."

I smiled sweetly, fastening my coat. "My dear, if I wanted a stage, I'd have charged admission."

Amira shook her head, but her lips twitched. "Don't push it, Victoria."

I stepped out into the street, heart racing, cheeks flushed. I hadn't felt this alive in years.

Rules were all well and good. But sometimes, breaking them was half the fun.

✦ ✦ ✦

Chapter 6

The Line Break

I had promised myself I wouldn't linger after my meeting, but my feet betrayed me. One glance at the discreet black door and I was inside again, brushing past Amira with a guilty smile.

Daniel Carter was there, of course. Same chair. Same jacket. Dial on red.

He looked up as I entered, the faintest spark in his eyes. I felt the heat of it across the room.

This time, I didn't hesitate. I poured my coffee, walked straight to his table, and turned his dial to green with a single flick of my finger.

"Cheeky," he murmured.

"I warned you," I said, settling into the chair opposite. "Dangerous habit."

We talked— the kind of talk that danced along a knife-edge. I teased him about his court days, about the wig I imagined he must have worn while dismantling witnesses. He teased me about being a business tyrant in heels, conquering boardrooms by breakfast.

It was when I leaned forward, hair falling over one shoulder, that his composure cracked. His eyes dipped, just for a moment, to the hint of cleavage my blouse betrayed.

I caught him, smiling like a cat. "Mr Carter," I whispered, "you really must learn to respect the evidence."

He laughed softly, and the sound curled inside me.

But it was what happened next that changed everything.

I reached across, under the pretext of brushing a crumb from the table, and let my fingers graze his hand. Barely a second. A touch so light it could have been accidental.

The air between us shifted.

Neither of us spoke for a long moment. Then Daniel folded his paper, laid it aside, and said in a voice lower than before:

"This is a very dangerous game we're playing, Ms Jennings."

I tilted my head. "Then why are you still sitting here?"

We lasted another ten minutes, keeping up the pretence of conversation, before Amira appeared with the quiet efficiency of a stage manager closing the curtains. Her eyes flicked from me to Daniel, then to our dials, then back again.

"Perhaps," she said, voice cool but amused, "you two might consider taking this particular discussion… elsewhere."

I rose gracefully, smoothing my skirt. "Excellent idea."

Daniel stood too, holding the door open for me. The street air felt colder, sharper.

We walked a few paces in silence, until I stopped. "Well then," I said.

He turned toward me. "Well then."

And just like that, I kissed him. Not soft, not tentative. A deliberate, claiming kiss that made his hand find the small of my back and pull me closer.

When we broke apart, my lipstick was smudged, his composure cracked, and my pulse racing.

"Mr Carter," I said, breathless but smiling, "consider the rules officially broken."

He laughed, low and hungry. "Then let's see how far you're willing to break them."

I linked my arm through his. "Careful. You might find out I have no limits at all."

The Apartment

I unlocked the door to my flat and stepped aside, gesturing for Daniel to enter. He hesitated just long enough for me to grin. 'Good', I thought, 'he knows he's about to be devoured.'

I closed the door behind us, kicked off my heels, and leaned back against the wood, arms folded, watching him take in the room.

"Well then," I said, voice low, "shall we dispense with the polite bit?"

Before he could answer, I caught him by the tie and yanked him hard enough that his mouth crashed against mine. His hands came to my waist instinctively, gripping, steadying, but I was already biting his lower lip, forcing him to respond, making it clear I wasn't after tenderness.

He groaned into my mouth, and that was my victory. I pushed him back toward the sofa, guiding him with my grip on his tie like he was on a leash.

"Sit," I ordered.

He did.

I straddled him in a single motion, skirt riding high, blouse falling open as I pressed against him. I rolled my hips deliberately, dragging a groan out of his throat, and laughed softly against his ear.

"Barrister Carter," I whispered, "you argue beautifully. But I think I prefer you like this."

My nails scraped down his chest as I tugged his shirt open, buttons pinging free. I kissed down his throat, biting just enough to make him shudder, then looked up at him, hair wild, eyes blazing.

"You like control, don't you?" I teased, fingers wrapping around his wrists and pinning them back against the sofa. "All those years cross-examining, intimidating. But here?" I ground down on him, slow and hard. "Here you do what I say."

He tried to speak, but I cut him off with another bruising kiss, swallowing the sound, biting his tongue before pulling back with a wicked smile.

"That's better," I purred.

From there, I set the pace with ruthless precision. I undid his belt and freed him, stroking, teasing, deliberately holding back, enjoying the twitch of his jaw as he fought not to beg.

"Relax," I murmured. "I'm going to ruin you."

I shifted, lowered myself onto him slowly, inch by inch, watching his composure splinter. His head fell back, a low curse escaping, and I smiled triumphantly.

"Yes," I whispered, rocking hard, faster now. "That's the sound I wanted."

My hands tangled in his hair, my hips relentless, every movement claiming, daring, taunting. I rode him with the same confidence I used in boardrooms — unapologetic, commanding, unstoppable.

He tried to regain control, hands grabbing my waist, thrusting up into me — but I only laughed, wild and breathless.

"Too late," I gasped, nails dragging down his chest. "You're mine tonight."

When I came, it was loud, unrestrained, my head thrown back as my body shook over him. Daniel followed, gripping me like he'd never let go, his own control shattering completely beneath me.

We collapsed together, breathless, slick with sweat, the silence of my flat broken only by the ragged sound of our breathing.

I leaned down, kissed his jaw, and whispered with a wicked grin:

"Well, Mr Carter. Consider yourself cross-examined."

Chapter 7
The Warning

Daniel hadn't been in for four days. Four bloody days.

I told myself I didn't care, that I was enjoying the peace, the solitude, the uninterrupted coffee. But I still caught myself glancing at his chair every time I walked in. Empty. Linen jacket nowhere in sight. Perhaps he'd melted into a puddle of barrister smugness and Amira had mopped him up.

On the fifth day, I stopped pretending I wasn't restless.

That's when I noticed him.

Not Daniel. Someone else.

Younger — early forties, maybe. Dark hair, jaw like something off a grooming advert, and a shirt that said 'yes, this was expensive, and no, you can't buy it on the high street.' He didn't bother with the usual props — no laptop, no newspaper. He just sat there watching me.

Not in a creepy way. In a curious way. And I liked it.

So I did what any sensible woman would do: I flipped my dial to green.

His mouth curved into a slow smile. He flipped his to green too, no hesitation. Brave boy.

I leaned back in my chair, let my hair fall to one side, toyed with the handle of my coffee cup like it was something far more interesting. He kept watching. I liked that too.

Maybe too much.

Because in Deep Blend, you don't perform. You don't preen. You don't make it obvious. It's not that sort of place. And I… may have forgotten myself.

By the time I crossed one leg over the other — deliberately slow, hemline slipping a fraction higher — I noticed two other members looking over. One woman by the bookshelves actually flipped her dial to red so firmly it clanged.

And then Amira appeared.

She doesn't walk so much as glide, like she's been trained by the Secret Service. One minute she isn't there, the next she's standing at your elbow with a tablet and a look that could kill small animals.

"Ms Jennings," she said, voice low and silk-smooth. "Might I have a word?"

I gave her my sweetest innocent smile. "Of course."

She led me toward the cloakroom corridor. My heels echoed far too loudly, like the world's most guilty woman.

"Deep Blend," she began, "is not a stage. Nor is it a marketplace. Members come here for privacy. For quiet. For dignity."

"Amira, darling, I wasn't—"

"You were." She didn't raise her voice. She didn't need to. "Not egregiously. But enough that others noticed. This is your first warning. There won't be a second."

I considered a witty retort, something about being old enough not to be scolded. But instead, I smirked and said, "Well, that's delicious. A formal warning at my age. I feel positively scandalous."

Her eyes softened slightly. "You're clever, Victoria. Don't pretend otherwise. Just remember where you are."

And with that, she glided off again, leaving me leaning against the paneling, half-amused, half-aroused by the sheer authority of the woman.

When I returned to my seat, Adonis-With-the-Jawline was still watching. I gave him a little smile — wicked, deliberate — then flicked my dial back to red.

Game over.

For now.

As I left, I whispered to myself: 'Well, Vicky, congratulations. You've become the café flirt. And Amira's onto you.'

The thought made me laugh all the way home.

✦ ✦ ✦

Chapter 8

Silent Signals

I wasn't supposed to be back the next day.

After Amira's little lecture, I should have stayed away, given it a week, maybe two, let the air clear. But patience has never been my strong suit. Especially not when there's a man with shoulders like carved oak and eyes that follow me like I'm the last chocolate truffle in the box.

So I went back. Of course I did.

This time, I wasn't going to use words.

I chose my usual seat, set my dial to green — restraint, or the appearance of it — and poured my coffee slowly, letting my sleeve slip low enough to show a whisper of wrist and forearm. It's extraordinary what men notice when you let them.

He was already there. Dark hair, crisp shirt, green dial glowing in invitation. He wasn't reading, wasn't pretending. He was waiting. For me.

I crossed my legs deliberately. Not enough to scandalise anyone else, but enough to let my hem rise an inch too high. A slow adjustment, a tilt of my knee — and there it was: the black lace edge of my stocking. Barely a flicker, a glimpse. A half-second invitation he couldn't mistake.

His reaction was delicious. His jaw tightened, his hand froze around his cup. He didn't blink.

Good boy.

I let my hand wander across the table, fingers trailing over the wood in lazy circles. Then, as though absentminded, I reached for the candle holder — a simple brass piece with a white stub of wax. My fingers wrapped around it, stroking up and down the stem, slow, rhythmic, as though I wasn't even aware of what I was doing.

I knew exactly what I was doing.

To anyone else, it was fidgeting. To him, it was unmistakable.

I didn't look at him directly. That would have been far too obvious. Instead, I let my eyes skim the page of my book, pretending to read while my fingers slid, curled, caressed the brass. A deliberate pace. A secret performance for an audience of one.

And oh, he was watching.

His lips parted slightly. He leaned forward in his chair, elbows resting on his knees, dial glowing green between us like a signal light. His coffee sat cooling, forgotten. Every line of his body was taut with focus, tethered to the movement of my hand.

I shifted again, just slightly, letting the hem of my skirt ride higher as though I hadn't noticed. Another flash of lace. My thighs pressed together, slow, deliberate, as I ran my thumb along the rim of the candle holder.

I bit my lip, feigning concentration on the words in front of me, though I couldn't have said what book I'd opened.

I was writing my own story now. And he was hanging on every page.

Of course, it couldn't last. Nothing ever does in Deep Blend.

I felt it before I saw her — Amira's presence, gliding across the floor like a shadow. She didn't speak. She didn't need to. She just stood by the far counter, eyes flicking briefly toward me, then toward him, then down at the dials.

A reminder.

A warning.

I let my hand slip casually away from the candle holder, smoothed my skirt, and flicked my dial back to red with a neat little click.

When I dared glance back, he was smiling. Not smug, not mocking — but a small, private smile, the kind that said: 'message received.'

And that was enough.

For today.

Chapter 9
The Restroom Rule

I told myself I wouldn't push it again.

After the candle incident — after Amira's eyes drilling into me like a nun with a ruler — I promised myself I'd behave. Drink my coffee, read my book, keep my legs crossed like a respectable woman.

That lasted all of ten minutes.

Because he was there again. Dark hair, jawline like a chisel, and that shirt, the dial glowing green before I'd even taken my seat. And those eyes. Always those eyes — watching me as if the whole café was just set dressing around our little show.

I sipped my coffee, tried to read, failed miserably. The air between us was too taut, humming with a private current. I felt it on my skin, in my stomach, lower. It was unbearable.

So I made the decision.

I stood, slowly, adjusting my skirt as though nothing at all was unusual. I didn't look at him. Didn't need to. I walked toward the corridor that led to the restrooms, each click of my heels on the polished wood like punctuation.

The air shifted. I knew he was following.

The ladies' room was empty, the faint lavender scent of polish and soap lingering in the stillness. I let the door swing shut behind me — soft, noiseless. My reflection in the mirror looked far too composed for how fast my heart was racing.

The handle turned again. Quietly. He slipped inside, closing it with careful precision. Our eyes met in the mirror. We didn't speak. Instead, I tilted my head slightly, a silent command. He obeyed.

I reached back, caught his tie in my fist, and pulled him against me. Our mouths met hard, desperate, but controlled — muffled groans, breath against breath, heat building in silence. My back pressed to the cool marble edge of the sinks, his body pinning me there.

The kiss deepened, teeth clashing, tongues tasting, my hands already tearing at his shirt, his fingers gripping my waist as though he'd lose me otherwise. Every sound was suppressed: gasps swallowed, moans caught in throats, bodies colliding in muted urgency.

We moved, unspoken agreement guiding us toward the cubicle. No slamming. No noise. Just the quiet click of the lock sliding home.

Inside, the world shrank. A narrow box of heat and tension.

He pushed my skirt up with shaking hands, my knickers torn down with swift precision. His lips at my neck, my nails clawing at his shoulders. Every thrust of movement was metered, stifled, like a storm forced into silence.

"God," he whispered, barely audible, breath hot against my ear.

"Shut up and fuck me" I hissed back, my body arching against him.

And then it happened — carnal, desperate, restrained only by necessity. He entered me hard, deep, each motion driving me against the cubicle wall with muted force. My hand clamped over my own mouth, muffling the cries that threatened to spill. His face buried in my neck, groaning low into my skin.

Every muscle burned with the effort of staying quiet. Every flicker of pleasure was amplified by the danger of being overheard.

My climax hit sharp and fast, rolling through me in waves I barely kept contained, nails digging into his back, teeth sinking into his shoulder. He followed almost instantly, body shuddering, his muffled groan vibrating against my throat as he came deep inside me.

For a moment, there was nothing but the sound of our breathing — ragged, uneven, filling the tiny cubicle.

Then a soft laugh escaped me, wicked and satisfied. "Well," I whispered, lips brushing his ear, "that was far better than a cappuccino."

We composed ourselves in silence. Straightening clothes, fixing hair, disguising the wreckage of what had just happened. His shirt was ruined, my stockings shredded, my lipstick smeared. We didn't care.

We slipped out one at a time, careful, silent. Back into the hush of Deep Blend, as though nothing at all had happened.

But when I caught his eye across the room again, his mouth curved into that same knowing smile.

And I knew we'd both be back for more.

Chapter 10
The Rekindling

I'd forgotten what it felt like.

Desire, I mean. Not the polite sort you can tidy up with a vibrator in ten minutes before bed, but the kind that lingers in your body for days. The sort that makes you restless at meetings, distracted in the supermarket, wet just from remembering the way a man looked at you across a room.

Deep Blend has woken me up.

It wasn't supposed to. I told myself it was just a sanctuary. A place to sit in peace, drink coffee, remind myself I wasn't the only woman in London still single past fifty. Nothing dangerous, nothing dramatic.

And yet here I am — sprawled in bed, silk robe slipping open, one hand resting over my breasts, the other between my thighs, replaying every second of the last week like a favourite film.

Daniel first. That kiss outside the café, the way his composure cracked when I straddled him, his precious tie bunched in my fist while I rode him until he swore like a dockworker. God, the thrill of taking apart a man who thought he couldn't be undone.

Then yesterday. Dark-hair. The restroom. The way he followed without hesitation, no words, no questions. Just heat and hunger and my back pressed to the cubicle wall as we fucked in silence, muffling our own cries like teenagers sneaking around.

The memory makes me ache all over again.

I slip my fingers lower, already slick, already needy, circling slow and deliberate. My robe falls fully open now, breasts exposed, nipples tight as I picture his hands on me — rough, desperate — while I whispered for him to be quiet, quiet, quiet. The danger of it, the delicious risk, makes my hips lift to meet my own hand.

"Oh, Vicky," I murmur to myself, biting my lip. "You wicked woman."

I think of both of them at once. Daniel's sharp wit and steady hands, the other man's raw   urgency, the way I was the common denominator — the one in control, the one who started it, fed it, took what I wanted.

My pace quickens, breath hitching, thighs trembling as the pleasure builds. I press harder, faster, imagining a new pair of eyes across the café, another dial flipped green, another secret waiting to be broken.

The climax hits hard, my body arching, shuddering, a muffled cry spilling into the pillow as I come in waves that leave me shaking and grinning at the same time.

I collapse back against the sheets, robe tangled, hair wild. My heart thunders, my body glows.

And all I can think, wickedly, smugly, is this:

'Deep Blend has ruined me. And I've never been so grateful.'

Chapter 11
The Seminar Surprise

I hadn't gone to the seminar looking for anything except a strong coffee and maybe the odd idea worth stealing. "Leadership in Transition" — the kind of thing business owners attend to remind ourselves we're still relevant. A room full of suits, handouts, and those bloody clip-on microphones that make everyone sound like they're narrating a hostage video.

I took my seat, flicked through the glossy agenda, and tried not to yawn.

And then I saw him.

Dark hair. Clean jawline. Blue shirt this time, no tie. He was across the room, leaning casually against the wall like he owned it. Our eyes met, and it was instant. A jolt.

I nearly laughed out loud. Of all the places — here. Him. The man who'd had me pinned against a toilet cubicle only days ago.

He smiled. Small, private. Recognition and memory, all in one look.

I crossed my legs slowly, adjusting my skirt, letting the hem rise just a fraction. His eyes flickered down, just for a heartbeat, then back up to meet mine. My pulse quickened.

The seminar droned on — talk of strategy, alignment, "moving into the future." I hardly heard a word. Every time I looked up, he was watching me. That same heat simmered just beneath the polite surface, both of us reliving exactly what we'd done in silence, surrounded now by oblivious professionals with clipboards.

When the coffee break came, I wandered to the far corner deliberately, cup in hand. A moment later, he was beside me.

"Victora," he said softly, his voice more confident now than in the café. "I wondered if I'd see you again."

"You didn't seem to be wondering in the restroom," I murmured back, my lips curling.

He almost choked on his coffee, laughter muffled in his throat. "God, you're dangerous."

"Yes," I said. "And you like it."

His eyes flickered, then — there it was. A shift. A flash of something else. Not just lust, but hunger of a different flavour. A glint of… vulnerability?

"What is it?" I asked, lowering my voice.

He hesitated. "You'll laugh."

"Probably," I said. "But tell me anyway."

He leaned closer, his breath warm against my ear. "I… like being told what to do."

I blinked, then smiled slowly. 'Well, well.'

The restroom encounter replayed in my head, how he'd obeyed every subtle cue I'd given him without question. How he'd followed me into the ladies' without hesitation. How he'd melted under my hand when I gripped his tie.

A secret kink. Obedience. Submission.

And here he was, confessing it to me over conference coffee like we were discussing the weather.

I sipped my drink, letting the silence stretch. Then I tilted my head, eyes fixed on his.

"Stand up straighter," I said softly.

His spine snapped upright. Instinctive. Automatic.

A thrill rushed through me.

"Oh, this," I whispered, "is going to be fun."

A shiver ran through me. He wasn't bluffing.

We didn't linger in the conference hall. I slipped him a look, one that said 'follow me', and headed toward the side exit. No words. No questions. He obeyed without hesitation.

Outside, the city hummed, but I led him down the street, heels clicking, until we reached a boutique hotel two blocks away. He didn't ask. He just followed. Exactly as I wanted.

By the time the door closed behind us, I'd decided to play.

"Jacket off," I said.

He shrugged it free, draped it neatly over the chair.

"Shoes."

He toed them off instantly.

I walked around him slowly, like I was inspecting a prize. "Hands behind your back."

He did it. Just like that.

Oh, the thrill. The raw, wicked power of it.

I stepped closer, unbuttoned his shirt deliberately, one button at a time, brushing his skin with my nails as I went. His breath quickened, but he stayed still, arms locked behind him, waiting.

"Good boy," I murmured.

His jaw flexed, a faint tremor in his throat. That phrase had done something to him. I felt it. Saw it.

I smiled, leaning up to whisper against his ear. "You like it when I take control, don't you?"

"Yes," he breathed.

"Louder."

"Yes."

I tugged his shirt open fully, baring his chest, then pressed my palm flat against him. His heart hammered under my touch.

"On your knees."

He hesitated only half a beat before sinking down, the carpet soft beneath him, his eyes lifted to mine.

The sight nearly undid me. A strong, handsome man, obedient at my feet, waiting for instruction.

I slid my skirt higher, perched on the edge of the bed, and spread my legs just enough to show the lace tops of my stockings. His gaze locked there instantly, pupils blown wide.

"Touch me," I ordered. "Slowly. Only when I say."

His breath caught, his hands twitching, but he stayed frozen, waiting. The obedience made me ache.

I toyed with him for long minutes, giving small commands — "Closer. Stop. Look at me. Don't move." Each one he obeyed like scripture, his restraint trembling with need.

Finally, when I couldn't take it anymore, I leaned forward, tangled my fingers in his hair, and pulled his mouth to me.

The release was carnal, explosive — his obedience feeding my hunger, my control fuelling his desperation. Every moan was mine, every touch granted only by my permission.

And when it was over, when I lay back flushed and breathless, stockings askew, hair wild, he was still kneeling there, shirt open, eyes locked on me like a man who'd found his goddess.

"Oh," I whispered, laughing wickedly, "this is going to be my favourite seminar yet."

He was still kneeling, hands locked behind his back, eyes fixed on me like I was both temptation and torment. His chest rose and fell quickly, shirt hanging open, skin flushed.

I could feel the tremor in him — not fear, not doubt, but raw, aching anticipation. He wanted release. He wanted me. But more than that, he wanted permission.

I stroked his cheek with my fingertips, soft at first, then harder, making him look up at me. "You're not used to this, are you?"

"No," he admitted, breath catching. "But… it feels—"

"Say it."

"Right," he whispered. "It feels right."

The honesty made my stomach flip with wicked delight.

"Good boy," I purred. "Now keep your hands behind your back. Don't move. Not until I tell you."

I stood, slowly, deliberately, and stepped out of my skirt. His eyes flickered down instinctively — and I snapped my fingers. "Eyes up."

He obeyed instantly, jaw tightening, fighting himself. His body screamed to disobey, to look, to take — but he didn't. And that obedience made my pulse race.

"Look at you," I said, circling him slowly, running a nail along his shoulder. "Strong, clever, handsome. And all it takes is one word from me and you're trembling on the floor."

"Yes," he breathed, a shiver running through him.

I tugged at his hair, forcing his head back. "You like this. Being made to wait. Being told."

"Yes…" His voice cracked. His whole body vibrated with the effort of holding still.

I smiled. "Then you'll wait longer."

I slipped onto the bed, sat back against the pillows, and spread my thighs slowly, letting him see my lace and the heat between. His eyes widened, chest heaving, but he didn't move.

"See this?" I teased, running my fingers over myself, slow, deliberate. "You don't get it until I say. You can watch. You can ache. But you can't touch."

His breath grew ragged, hands fisting tight behind his back, body straining with denial. His arousal was obvious, pressing hard against his trousers, but still he didn't move.

"Oh, you're perfect," I whispered, circling myself faster, deliberately moaning, eyes locked on his. "You're shaking. You're desperate. And you're mine."

He groaned low in his throat, eyes dark, every ounce of him pleading silently.

I drew it out, pushing myself to the edge, letting him see me unravel while he knelt powerless, bound by my word. When my climax ripped through me, I cried out shamelessly, riding the waves, watching his face twist with hunger and frustration, his entire body taut with need.

When I finally came down, flushed and grinning, I beckoned him with one finger. "Come here."

He crawled forward instantly, hands still behind his back, like a man starved. I pulled him between my thighs, tangled my fingers in his hair, and finally gave him what he'd been aching for — permission.

The way he moaned when his mouth touched me was almost as sweet as the pleasure itself. Raw, grateful, devoted. Every flick of his tongue was worship, every sound muffled against me a confession.

And as I came again, harder, clutching his hair, thighs squeezing around his head, one thought blazed through me:

'Deep Blend gave me lust. But this man? He's given me power.'

◆ ◆ ◆

Chapter 12
Silent Control

The air changed the second I walked into Deep Blend.

I knew he was there before I saw him — that electric prickle along my skin, the weight of eyes already waiting for me. And there he was: dark hair, blue shirt today, dial glowing green. His posture perfect, but tense. Expectant.

I didn't go to him. Oh no. That would have ruined the game.

I slid into my usual seat, deliberately placing myself where he could see me but no one else would notice our line of sight. I set my dial to red, the signal that said 'not available' — but for him, that meant only one thing: control was mine.

I let him wait.

I opened my book, sipped my coffee, legs crossed elegantly. Then, with slow precision, I adjusted my skirt. Just an inch. Just enough lace flashing at the top of my stocking to catch his eye.

And it did. His jaw clenched. His throat bobbed. His hands tightened on his cup.

I raised one eyebrow, just slightly, and his whole body froze. Obedient.

Good boy.

I traced the rim of my coffee cup with one finger, round and round in slow circles. Then I lifted that finger to my mouth and sucked it clean, my eyes never leaving his.

The reaction was delicious — a shudder through his shoulders, a sharp exhale he tried to disguise. His hand twitched in his lap. He looked seconds away from moving.

I shook my head ever so slightly. 'Don't!'

His obedience was exquisite. His thighs tensed, his lips parted, but he stayed still.

I rewarded him by brushing my fingertips across the inside of my thigh, stopping just below the lace edge of my stocking. A languid caress, soft and wicked.

His pupils blew wide. He shifted in his chair, just barely, his chest heaving now as though each breath was a battle.

I leaned back, pretending to stretch, my hand sliding along the table's candle holder. Stroking the stem, up and down, slow, unmistakable. A rhythm that promised, teased, denied.

His face tightened, jaw locked, his body rigid. One hand gripped the saucer so hard I thought it might crack. The other twitched toward his lap, then curled into a fist.

I tapped the table once with my nail. 'Stop!'

He froze, shaking with the effort. His need was written all over him now: sweat at his temple, lips parted, eyes burning with hunger.

I slipped my fingers back into my mouth, slow and indulgent, then mouthed the words silently across the room: 'Good boy.'

And that was it.

I saw it. Felt it, almost — the rush that overtook him, the tremor through his body, the moment restraint shattered. His breath hitched sharp, his hips jerked once against the chair, and then the flush spread across his cheeks as he came in silence, right there in Deep Blend.

He closed his eyes for a second, lips pressed tight, fighting to stay composed. But I knew. I'd made him come without a touch. Without a word. From across the room.

I smiled, wicked and private, gathered my things, and stood.

Our eyes met one last time. His chest still heaving, his hands clenched in his lap, the faintest sheen of sweat on his brow. Ashamed? No. Exhilarated. Owned.

I leaned down as I passed, lips close to his ear but my voice barely a whisper:

"Next time, you'll ask permission."

Then I walked out, heels clicking, body humming with the thrill of power.

Outside, the cool evening air hit me, and I laughed softly to myself.

'Deep Blend wasn't just a café anymore. It was my theatre. And I'd just delivered my best performance yet.'

Chapter 13
The Silent Experiment

I needed to know.

The dark-haired man had already been halfway mine — primed, eager, submissive. But could I take a total stranger, a man who knew nothing of me, and make him surrender without a touch? Without a word?

I chose my stage carefully. A hotel bar. Low lights, chrome and glass polished to sterility, the clink of glasses and hum of business chatter. No one paying attention to anyone else.

He was perfect. Alone at a corner table, late forties maybe, sandy hair, confident in his suit but restless in his eyes. A man who had things under control — or thought he did.

I sat opposite. No greeting. Just presence. His gaze flicked up, caught mine, slid away. Then back. Hooked.

I let him wait.

First, a sip of wine. Slow. My tongue lingering on the rim of the glass, lips wrapping the stem as though it were something far thicker, far more indecent. His eyes darted down, then snapped back up, as though ashamed to be caught.

I smiled, secret and knowing.

I crossed my legs under the table, smooth, unhurried, letting my skirt slide higher until the lace of my stockings peeked into view. His breath hitched, faint but audible in the hush between conversations.

Good.

I leaned back, draped an arm across the chair, and let my other hand wander lazily across the table. My fingers found the stem of the candle holder. I began to stroke it — slow, deliberate, up and down, circling the top with a rhythm too intimate to mistake.

His lips parted. His hand tightened around his glass. The heat between us was growing, invisible but suffocating.

I slipped two fingers between my lips. Wet. Slow. I sucked them deeper, tongue curling, before drawing them out with a soft, obscene sound that made his knuckles whiten against the table.

Then I lowered that hand to my thigh. I dragged my fingers over the bare skin above my stocking, brushing closer to the edge of my skirt. My breathing shifted — heavier now, deliberately audible. I parted my lips slightly, then my thighs and slid two fingers up between them entering my wet pussy, eyes locked on his.

His reaction was exquisite. His chest rose faster, nostrils flaring, body taut as if every muscle fought restraint. His hips jerked once against the chair, subtle, but I caught it. His thighs pressed together hard.

I tilted my head, raising one brow. 'Stay still.'

The tension broke him.

His eyes fluttered shut for a fraction, mouth parting as a groan caught in his throat. His body jerked again — sharp, uncontrolled. And then it came: the stiffening of his shoulders, the tremor in his jaw, the unmistakable twitch of his hips as he came silently in his tailored trousers.

A hot flush spread across his cheeks. His hand gripped the table so tight his ring bit into the wood. He breathed raggedly, fighting to remain outwardly composed, but the truth was written in the tremble of his thighs, the wet darkness blooming against his control.

And I had done it.

Without a touch. Without a word.

I lifted my wine glass, sipped, and let a wicked smile curl my lips.

When I rose to leave, I didn't look back. I didn't need to.

I'd proven it.

It wasn't chance. It wasn't luck.
It was me.

✦ ✦ ✦

Chapter 14
Reflections

I didn't sleep that night.

Not because I was restless, but because I was buzzing. Every nerve in my body still alight with the memory of what I'd just done.

It had been so easy. Too easy.

A stranger. A man who hadn't spoken a single word to me, who hadn't touched me, who hadn't even known he'd been chosen. And yet, there I was — stroking my own fingers inside my wet cunt, hidden by nothing more than a carefully arranged skirt and the shadows of a hotel bar — and there he was, ejaculating in his trousers, silent, helpless, completely mine.

I laughed out loud in my bed, the sound wicked and satisfied. Who knew power could feel like this? Who knew it could be so… simple?

It wasn't luck. I knew that now. I'd unlocked something inside myself. A part of me that had been waiting all along. The wit, the teasing, the sharp tongue — they'd always been there. But this? This was a new me. A new Victora who could make a man come just by deciding he would.

I thought back to his face. That tremor in his jaw. The way he tried so hard to hold it back, to stay composed, until his body betrayed him completely. He hadn't stood a chance.

And what thrilled me most wasn't the act itself — though God, the wetness between my thighs reminded me it had been plenty thrilling — but the ease. No words. No touches. Just silent control, a theatre no one else noticed, played out right under their noses.

That thought made my nipples hard against the silk of my nightdress.

I slid my hand lower, still damp from reliving it all day, and whispered into the darkness: "You're mine, whoever you are. You didn't even know it, and you're mine."

The orgasm that followed wasn't gentle. It was sharp, fast, heady — the orgasm of a woman who has finally realised she doesn't just want power… she owns it.

When I collapsed back against the sheets, panting, hair clinging to my forehead, I smiled.

This was just the beginning.

✦ ✦ ✦

Chapter 15
Yesterday's News

I only popped in for ten minutes. A quick coffee between meetings, a breather before diving back into emails and contracts.

But Deep Blend has a way of reminding me where I started.

Daniel was there.

Sitting in his usual corner, hair perfectly combed, linen jacket, shirt crisp, dial a polite red. Reading something terribly worthy, no doubt. He didn't notice me at first — and that was the part that made me laugh. Once upon a time I'd hung on that man's glance, teased him into breaking his own composure, ridden him with glee until his sharp tongue begged.

Now? He was background. Wallpaper. A relic of the me who hadn't yet discovered what I could do.

I sat two tables away, coffee steaming, legs crossed. He still hadn't looked up. And I realised, with a little smirk, that I didn't care if he ever did.

Because Daniel had been fun. Amusing. A diversion. But Daniel needed reasons. Reasons to be undone, reasons to follow, reasons to crack his armor.

Me? I don't need reasons anymore.

I have power.

Real, dangerous, wet-between-the-thighs power. And Daniel, bless him, will never touch that side of me. Not now I've tasted more.

So I let him sit there, oblivious, his red dial glowing like a polite little 'no, thank you.' I sipped my coffee, remembering the stranger in the bar, remembering the dark-haired submissive on his knees, remembering how easy it had been to take what I wanted.

Daniel finally looked up. His eyes flickered, widened, that familiar little spark of interest. Once upon a time, my heart might have skipped.

Now, I just smiled faintly, a smile that said 'you missed your chance', and turned back to my coffee.

He didn't matter anymore.

Because I wasn't here for scraps. I was here to hunt.

✦ ✦ ✦

Chapter 16
Cracks in the Armor

It was only the flicker of an eye at first.

Amira. Always so composed, always immaculate behind her tablet, the guardian of Deep Blend. She was the one who caught me once, back in the early days, when my teasing was too obvious. A single look from her had been enough to freeze me in place.

But lately… her eyes linger differently.

She pretends she's just checking dials, polishing tables, monitoring the silence. But I feel it. That watchfulness. She's not looking at everyone anymore. She's looking at me.

And yesterday, I caught it.

The bar had been half-full, quiet as ever. I'd been sipping coffee, skirt a little higher than necessary, fingers toying with the rim of my cup. Across the room, a man shifted in his seat, his breathing just a fraction heavier. My little game was working, as always.

But it wasn't him I noticed.

It was Amira. Standing by the bookshelf, tablet in hand, eyes locked on me with something I'd never seen before. Not suspicion. Not disapproval.

Curiosity.

She looked away the moment our eyes met, jaw tightening, mask back in place. But the crack had shown.

Later, as I left, she caught my wrist lightly. A rare break in protocol.

"Victoria," she murmured, so soft I almost didn't hear. "You… do things. Things no one else here does."

I tilted my head, wicked smile tugging my lips. "Do I?"

Her eyes dropped, the faintest blush colouring her cheeks — Amira, always the ice queen. "I notice. That's all."

I leaned closer, voice a whisper. "Noticed… or intrigued?"

Her silence was answer enough.

I lifted her hand gently from my wrist, handed her my business card and walked out with my heels clicking on the polished floor, heart racing with a new thrill.

Because if there was one thing I'd never expected, it was this: the untouchable Amira, the woman who'd policed everyone else's desire, had just betrayed her own.

And I knew the look in her eyes.

Longing.

Hunger.

Loneliness dressed up as authority.

Amira hadn't touched anyone in years. I could see it now. But she'd been watching me — and what she wanted wasn't to scold.

She wanted to learn.

Chapter 17
The Call

I didn't expect her to actually use it.

When I slipped my number into Amira's palm as I left the café that day, I half-expected it to be forgotten. She was the guardian, the rule-keeper, the one who enforced silence and discretion with a single arch of her brow. Not the type to call a woman like me.

But three nights later, my phone lit up with an unfamiliar number.

"Victoria?"

Her voice was softer than I'd ever heard it. Almost shy.

"Yes," I said, stretching out the word, already smiling. "Amira."

There was a pause. A breath. "I was wondering…" She trailed off. "Could we meet? Not at the café. Somewhere else. Just for coffee."

Coffee. Yes, of course. Coffee.

"Of course," I said, as if this weren't deliciously intriguing. "When?"

"My break tomorrow," she replied quickly, as though she might lose courage if she didn't anchor it down. "There's a little place near the square. Quieter than most. Half one."

"I'll be there."

The next day, I arrived early. The café was nothing like Deep Blend — brighter, louder, filled with the clatter of cups and chatter of people who didn't care about dials or discretion. I chose a booth in the corner, waited.

When Amira arrived, she looked… different. Not immaculate. Not polished to perfection. Her blouse was simple, her hair softer, less armor and more woman. She glanced around nervously before sliding into the booth opposite me.

For the first time since I'd known her, she looked out of place. Vulnerable.

"Thank you for coming," she murmured, folding her hands too neatly in front of her.

I leaned back, studying her, enjoying the reversal. "I'm intrigued. What made you call me?"

Her eyes flickered to mine, then away. "I've been watching you. At Deep Blend. The way you… behave."

A wicked smile tugged at my lips. "Covertly misbehaving, you mean."

A flush rose in her cheeks. "Yes. That." She swallowed hard. "I haven't… been with anyone in years, Victoria. I've almost forgotten how it feels to… want. And then I saw you, and I thought—"

She broke off, biting her lip.

I leaned forward, lowering my voice. "You thought what?"

Her eyes finally met mine, wide and raw. "I thought maybe you could teach me."

When she whispered, "I thought maybe you could teach me," I felt the crackle in the air between us.

Amira, the woman who policed Deep Blend with an iron eyebrow, was sitting across from me like a girl on her first date. Vulnerable. Nervous. Longing.

I leaned back in my chair, swirling the dregs of my coffee, letting her words hang. "Teach you," I repeated, rolling the phrase across my tongue.

She nodded once, quickly, her composure slipping again. "Yes. I… don't know where to start."

"Good," I said, smiling wickedly. "Because starting is the hardest part."

Amira came to my flat after the café closed the next evening. I opened the door to find her standing there, out of uniform, out of armor. Simple blouse, plain trousers, flats. No sharp lines, no gloss. Just Amira, stripped of the mask she wore at Deep Blend.

I let her in, poured us wine, and waited. She perched nervously on the edge of my sofa, her hands folded too neatly in her lap.

"Lesson one," I said, standing before her. "Stop sitting like you're at confession. Unfold yourself. Own the space."

She hesitated, then shifted, stretching her legs a little, letting her arms relax at her sides. Already softer. Already more Amira.

"Better," I purred. "Lesson two: wear something that makes you feel like your body belongs to you, not to your job. Tomorrow, no blouses, no flats. A dress. Heels. Stockings if you dare."

Her lips parted. "Stockings?"

"Yes," I said, leaning down, my hand brushing lightly along her thigh. "There's nothing like the whisper of silk against your own skin to remind you you're alive and drive men crazy."

She shivered under my touch, a tremor she couldn't disguise.

"Lesson three," I went on, straightening. "Never apologise for desire. You've kept yourself in check for years, haven't you?"

She nodded faintly.

"Well, that ends here. With me, you don't hold back. You want? You take. Or, at the very least, you learn how to make them want so much they beg to give."

Her breath caught. "And you'll show me?"

I smiled, slow and certain. "I'll show you everything."

And so it began.

For a week, every night after the café had closed, Amira came to me. Each evening, another lesson.

How to walk in heels, not like armor but like invitation.
How to sit with a skirt so the lace of stockings showed
only if you wanted it to.
How to hold a wine glass by the stem, turning a sip into
a promise.
How to meet a man's eyes just long enough to undo
him, then look away before he can recover.

We laughed. God, we laughed. At her first wobbles in
borrowed stilettos. At her shocked gasp when I showed
her how to bite her lip just so. At the way she flushed
when I made her practise tracing the rim of a glass with
her tongue.

But beneath the humour was something sharper. Each
night I watched her armor peel away, layer by layer. She
was hungry. Desperate for intimacy after years of cold
solitude. And every lesson, every little command, lit her
from the inside out.

By the end of the week, Amira wasn't just learning. She
was becoming.

And as I stood behind her in the mirror on the seventh
night, her body wrapped in black lace, her posture
confident, her smile wicked for the first time — I
thought to myself:

'I've created something dangerous. And she doesn't
even know it yet.'

✦ ✦ ✦

Chapter 18
Into the Field

By the end of our week together, Amira looked nothing like the woman who had first perched nervously on my sofa.

Tonight, she was mine to unveil.

I chose the venue carefully — a jazz lounge tucked beneath one of the city's better hotels. Low lights, velvet booths, soft brass humming in the background. The kind of place where people came to drink slowly and watch each other without admitting it.

When Amira arrived, my breath caught.

She'd obeyed every instruction. Black silk dress, cut just high enough to promise, just low enough to tempt. Stockings — yes, she'd dared — with the faintest hint of lace showing when she crossed her legs. Her hair, usually pinned tight, fell loose around her shoulders. Her lipstick a deep, sinful red.

She was still Amira — poised, immaculate — but there was something new in her eyes. A flicker of mischief.

"Lesson eight," I whispered as I kissed her cheek in greeting. "Remember: every man in this room is already wondering about you. All you have to do is choose which one to let wonder longer."

We slid into a booth, ordered wine, and watched.

It didn't take long. A man at the bar, maybe early fifties, tall, silver at the temples. Well-dressed, well-fed, the kind of man used to being noticed. And he noticed Amira.

I leaned closer. "Now show me."

She hesitated only a second before turning slightly in her seat, letting her legs shift, the silk of her dress falling just enough to reveal lace. She lifted her glass, held his gaze over the rim as she drank, then set it down with a deliberate drag of her fingertip around the stem.

The man's eyes flared. He shifted on his stool, trying to mask it.

My pulse raced. She was doing it.

Amira turned back to me, lips curving with a secret smile. "He's watching," she murmured.

"Of course he is," I said. "Because you're making him."

Over the next twenty minutes, I coached her in whispers, guiding her gestures — how to cross and uncross her legs with just enough pause, how to let her fingers linger at her throat, how to break eye contact and then reclaim it with devastating timing.

The man at the bar was unravelling before us. His glass forgotten, his posture shifting, his hunger barely hidden.

And Amira? She was glowing.

The woman who once folded herself tight behind rules was now spreading her power across the room, silent, magnetic, devastating.

I squeezed her hand under the table, my voice low and wicked.

"You see it now, don't you? What it feels like to be the one in control. To know you could make him come without ever touching him."

Her smile deepened, eyes glinting.

"Yes," she whispered. "I want more."

Chapter 19

Sanctified Sins

If I was going to call myself a master, I needed more than willing men in dim bars.

I needed resistance.

I needed to take someone who didn't want to want me, and break him anyway.

Which is why I went to the church.

Afternoon light poured through stained glass, dust motes turning the air into something holy. Candles flickered in their brass holders. A few scattered figures whispered prayers. And him.

A man alone in the back pew, back straight, hands clasped tight. He had the look of a true believer — the rigid posture, the furrowed brow, lips moving silently as though bargaining with God.

The perfect challenge.

I slipped into the pew across the aisle from him. My heels clicked once against the stone,   deliberately loud in the hush. His eyes flicked to me, then away, sharp and disapproving.

Good. Let him scorn me. Let him think I didn't belong here.

Because in a moment, he'd know whose temple he truly prayed at.

I crossed my legs slowly, silk stockings whispering against each other, my skirt riding just high enough to show lace. His jaw tightened, though his eyes stayed stubbornly fixed on the altar.

I leaned back, sighing as if in prayer, and let my hand slide onto my thigh. At first innocent, resting lightly. Then higher. Stroking the lace. Tugging the fabric. A rhythm forming.

I saw it: the quick dart of his eyes, the immediate snap back upward, the flush creeping into his neck.

I parted my lips, let out a soft sound — half-moan, half-exhale — that echoed indecently in the holy air. His lips froze mid-prayer. His fingers clenched harder.

He hated it. He wanted to resist.

And yet.

I let my hand slide between my thighs, discreet but unmistakable. My hips shifted, my breath catching louder, more shameless. The pew creaked beneath me as I moved.

His eyes flicked again. This time they lingered.

Our gazes locked. His was fury and hunger tangled into one. I smiled, slow, wicked, sliding two fingers deeper into myself beneath the shadow of my skirt.

His lips pressed together in a grimace. His nostrils flared. His shoulders trembled with the effort of stillness.

"Forgive me," he mouthed silently toward the altar —
but his eyes stayed on me.

I spread my thighs wider, letting the silk stretch, making
sure he saw. My fingers moved harder now, my chest
rising with the rhythm, my other hand caressing one
breast, my mouth falling open as I rode the edge
shamelessly.

He broke.

His body stiffened, his hands clutching the pew in front
of him. His jaw slackened, a stifled groan catching in his
throat. His hips jerked once, twice. And then it was
done.

Release.

Right there, in his place of worship.

I pulled my hand free, glistening, and sucked my fingers
slowly, never breaking eye contact. His face twisted —
disgust and devastation warring with the undeniable
truth of what had just happened.

I stood, smoothed my skirt, and walked down the aisle
with my heels echoing like a hymn.

Outside, the air was crisp and pure against my flushed
skin. I laughed softly to myself, wicked triumph curling
in my chest.

'If I can corrupt the devout in his own church, then
yes… I'm ready to teach Amira.'

Chapter 20
The Confession

It came out of her like a dam breaking.

We were back at my flat, wine glasses empty, the city buzzing faintly beyond the windows. Amira sat curled on my sofa in the lace dress I'd insisted on, her cheeks flushed not from drink but from something heavier.

"Victoria," she said suddenly, her voice low, urgent. "I need to tell you what I really want."

I tilted my head, smiling. "Go on."

Her hands twisted in her lap, but her eyes met mine with raw honesty. "It's not just about making them want. Not just the teasing or the power. What I want…" She drew a shaky breath. "What I want is for a man to take me. To take me so completely I can't think, can't breathe, can't… be myself. I want to be fucked senseless. Used. Until I can't hold back anymore."

Her words hit me like a spark to tinder.

So that was it. That was the hunger behind her eyes. Not just curiosity. Not just the thrill of copying my games. Amira, who spent years folded into professionalism, into silence, into control, didn't want more control. She wanted the opposite.

She wanted obliteration. I leaned forward, brushing my fingers over hers. "So you don't want to be the teacher. You want to be the lesson."

Her breath caught. "Yes."

"And you don't just want desire," I murmured, my lips brushing her ear. "You want to be taken. Fucked. Made to forget who you are."

Her eyes closed, her body shuddering at the word. "Yes."

I sat back, studying her. A woman who had denied herself for years. A woman who wore composure like armor. And now, at last, she was peeling it off, piece by piece, laying herself bare in front of me.

"Then that," I said softly, "is what we'll find for you."

Her eyes opened, wide and shining.

I smiled, wicked and knowing. "I'll teach you how to attract him. I'll teach you how to hold him. And when the right man comes along — I'll make sure he fucks you until you can't even remember your own name."

Amira trembled, not with fear, but with anticipation. For the first time since I'd known her, she wasn't composed. She wasn't the guardian, the rule-keeper, the polished professional.

She was a woman.

Hungry. Desperate. Ready.

And I thought to myself: 'this might be the most dangerous lesson of all.'

✦ ✦ ✦

Chapter 21
The Lesson of Three

I promised Amira I would find her a man.

Not the wrong kind — not some fumbling stranger who'd paw at her until she shut down again. No, I would choose him. Shape the encounter. Control the pace so she could step in or stay back, safe but aroused, with no pressure to do anything she didn't want.

It had to be her lesson, not her test.

I picked him carefully. A tall, broad-shouldered man I'd met twice before at a gallery opening — bold enough to follow my lead, discreet enough not to boast afterward. When I messaged him, he agreed instantly.

Tonight. My flat. You'll do as I say.

And so he came.

When Amira opened the door and saw him standing there — dark hair, hungry eyes — her breath caught. She looked at me, not him, her face flushed with nerves and something else.

I brushed my fingers down her arm. "Remember," I whispered, "you don't have to do anything. Just watch. Feel. Step in when it feels right."

She nodded, swallowing hard.

I led him to the sofa. Pushed him down. Straddled him before he could even breathe. My lips crashed against his, my hands sliding into his shirt, nails dragging over his chest. His groan vibrated against my mouth as I ground against him, already wet and throbbing.

But my eyes were on Amira.

She stood by the wall, frozen, watching me ride him with a hunger she didn't yet know how to name. I spread myself wider on him, letting my skirt ride high, stockings gleaming, my body shameless in its rhythm.

"See, Amira?" I moaned, throwing my head back so my throat arched, my tits straining against lace. "This is how you take what you want."

Her lips parted. Her hands clenched at her sides. She took one slow step closer.

I kissed him hard again, my tongue claiming his, then pulled back to whisper against his lips: "Don't touch her. Only me. Until she comes to you."

He nodded, breathless, obeying instantly.

I slid down, unzipping him, freeing his cock. My hand wrapped tight, stroking slow, teasing him while I turned my gaze on Amira. "Look at him. Look how ready he is for us."

Her eyes widened, fixed on the hard length in my hand, the shine of precum on my fingers. She bit her lip, trembling, caught between fear and desire.

I pressed the head of his cock against my wet pussy, gasping as I sank down onto him in one slow, merciless stroke. My moan filled the room, shameless, carnal.

"Oh, fuck yes."

Amira made a sound then. A tiny, involuntary gasp.

I smiled through the pleasure, hips rolling against him as I fucked him deeper, harder, faster. "Come closer," I said to her, my voice a velvet command. "Don't touch if you're not ready. Just watch. Watch me fuck him. Watch what you've been craving."

And she did.

She came closer. Close enough that I could reach out, take her hand, place it lightly against my thigh so she could feel the tremors of my body as I rode him.

Her eyes were wide, her lips parted, her breath coming faster.

I threw my head back and screamed my pleasure, using his body shamelessly, riding him until the sofa shook, until I felt the orgasm cresting sharp and unstoppable. And Amira's hand tightened on my leg, trembling, caught in the heat of it.

I came with a cry, clenching around him, soaking him, shuddering through waves of wicked delight.

And when I finally collapsed forward, panting, lips pressed to his ear, I whispered: "Now, Amira. If you want him… he's yours."

I looked up at her, flushed and trembling, poised between fear and longing.

Her eyes met mine.

And I knew: this was the lesson she'd been waiting for.

For a moment, she hovered — trembling, breathing too fast, her hand still gripping my thigh like she needed my pulse to steady her own.

Then she moved.

Slow at first, her eyes locked on mine as if asking permission. I gave her a single nod, wicked and approving. And that was all it took.

She lowered herself between his legs, her hands brushing his thighs. He looked at me for guidance, desperate, straining to hold back. I held his jaw and whispered, "Don't move. She needs to do this herself."

Amira's fingers wrapped around him. Tentative at first, then firmer, stroking along the hard, slick length I'd left glistening with my arousal. Her lips parted, and she leaned down, tongue flicking over the swollen head.

He groaned, loud, guttural, his hips jerking before I shoved him back down with a warning glare.

Amira gasped at his reaction, but then—oh, she smiled. A hungry, wicked little smile that told me she'd just discovered something she never wanted to give up again.

She took him deeper into her mouth, her hand pumping as she sucked, her eyes fluttering shut as though the act itself was rewiring her body. Years of restraint, of denying herself touch and heat, poured out of her in wet, desperate slurps that made him grip the cushions like his life depended on it.

I slid behind her, hands on her shoulders, guiding her rhythm, whispering in her ear: "Yes, that's it. Take him. Own him. Make him lose control."

She moaned around his cock, the vibration dragging another tortured groan from his throat.

And then she pulled back, wiping her mouth with the back of her hand, her chest heaving. She looked at me, eyes wide, wild.

"I need him inside me."

The words were ragged, urgent, undeniable.

I grinned, kissed her hard, tasting him on her lips, before pulling her up onto the sofa. I guided her body over him, my hands steadying her trembling thighs as she lowered herself onto his glistening hard cock.

The moment he filled her, she cried out — loud, raw, years of longing tearing free from her throat. She gripped his shoulders, riding down onto him with a desperation that was nothing like the careful, restrained Amira I'd known.

I held her hips, rocking her faster, harder, teaching her through motion, through rhythm, through my own wicked moans.

"Yes, Amira. That's it. Take him. Take what you've been craving."

She fucked him like she'd been starving for years —
because she had. Every thrust dragged a new sound
from her, every movement made her body shake with a
mix of shock and delight.

Her climax built fast, overwhelming her. I felt it in the
shudder of her thighs, the way her nails dug into his
chest, the way her breath caught in jagged gasps.

When it hit, it was violent. Squirting cum. She
screamed, collapsing forward, body clenching around
him as her orgasm ripped through her like a storm
finally breaking.

And I held her there, guiding her through it, whispering
wicked praise into her ear.

"You see now, don't you? This is what you wanted.
This is what it means to surrender."

✦ ✦ ✦

Chapter 22
The Hunt Together

Amira didn't wait long to ask.

Two nights after the threesome, she turned up at my flat again, out of uniform, her hair loose, her lips tinted crimson. She didn't even bother with small talk — she sat down, glass of wine untouched, and blurted:

"I want to do it again. Another one. But with you there."

Her eyes burned, not nervous this time, but resolute. "I felt safe because you were there, Victoria. I could let go because you were in control. I want that again."

I smiled, slow, predatory. "Then we'll hunt."

We chose a high-end cocktail bar in the city. The kind of place filled with men who wore their wealth in cufflinks and cologne, who thought they could buy attention as easily as another round of martinis.

But tonight, they were ours.

Amira looked devastating. Black pencil dress hugging her curves, heels that made her legs a weapon, and the kind of smoky eye that turned her into temptation incarnate. I'd trained her well.

We sat at the bar, side by side, sipping slowly, scanning. It didn't take long before one caught us — tall, late thirties, jawline sharp enough to cut glass, his navy suit tailored within an inch of its life. His confidence filled the space before he even spoke.

I leaned toward Amira. "What do you think?"

She smirked. "Perfect."

I gave the man a glance that lingered just long enough, then returned to my drink. He took the bait.

Within minutes he was leaning against the bar, ordering us champagne, making confident small talk. But the real conversation was in the way Amira licked the rim of her glass, in the way I brushed my hand against her thigh, in the way his eyes flicked between us with a hunger he couldn't disguise.

He thought he'd found two women to conquer. He had no idea he was being led.

We brought him back to my flat. The door barely closed before I pushed him against it, kissing him hard, my nails dragging down his chest. Amira stood back at first, watching, biting her lip, her eyes wide with that mixture of awe and hunger.

Then I beckoned.

"Come here, Amira."

She stepped forward, her hand sliding over his jaw, her lips brushing his. He groaned into her mouth, his cock already straining against his trousers.

I dropped to my knees, unzipping him, pulling him free. He was thick, hard, pulsing in my hand. I stroked him slowly, deliberately, while looking up at Amira.

"Your turn," I murmured.

Her eyes locked on mine as she lowered herself, lips parting, tongue flicking over his length before she swallowed him deep. His head hit the wall with a thud, his groan raw, guttural.

I guided her rhythm, stroking his shaft as she sucked, my other hand sliding under her dress, stroking her wetness through silk. She moaned around him, the vibration making his knees buckle.

And then I pulled her up, kissed her hard, tasting him on her lips. "Now we fuck him together."

I pushed him onto the sofa. Straddled him first, sinking down onto his cock with a shameless cry. Amira knelt behind me, kissing my shoulders, sliding her hands down to guide my hips as I rode him. Then I slipped off, pulling Amira into my place.

She gasped as he filled her, louder, rawer than before, her nails raking his chest. I leaned in, kissing her while he fucked up into her, hard and relentless. Her moans spilled into my mouth, desperate, unrestrained, her body shaking with every thrust.

We took turns — me straddling his face while Amira rode his cock, then swapping, using him like he was nothing more than our toy. His orgasms came ragged, muffled between our cries, his body wrecked while we still burned, insatiable.

Amira came twice that night, screaming the second, her face buried in my neck as I whispered, "Yes, that's it, let him fuck you senseless, just like you wanted."

By the time it was over, he was collapsed, drained, trembling. And we were sprawled together, tangled in silk and sweat, laughing like schoolgirls who'd set fire to the rules.

Amira's eyes glowed in the dark.

"Victora," she whispered, still breathless, "I don't ever want to stop."

I kissed her hair, smiling wickedly. "Good. Because neither do I."

✦ ✦ ✦

Chapter 23
The Show

Amira and I had crossed a line.

It wasn't just about men anymore. It wasn't just about teaching her to open herself, or finding the right body for her to surrender to. Somewhere between the lessons and the hunts, she and I had started devouring each other.

Her mouth on my cunt had become an addiction. Her fingers inside me, her wetness on my tongue — the way we drank each other like wine, greedy, shameless, desperate.

And we both realised something: men were no longer our masters, no longer even our partners. They were our audience.

So our next conquest wasn't chosen for his cock. He was chosen for his eyes.

We brought him to my flat — a man in his forties, polite, decent, the type who'd never expect what was about to happen. We made the rules clear the moment he walked in.

"You don't touch us," I said, my voice firm. "You sit. You watch. And if you're lucky, you come. Understand?"

He nodded, breathless, already hard in his trousers.

Amira and I led him to the armchair by the window, pushing him down into it like a throne. Then we stood before him, side by side, the two of us in lace and silk, our eyes locked on him as we let our dresses fall to the floor.

His jaw dropped.

And then the show began.

I kissed Amira first, slow, deep, our tongues tangling, her moan spilling into my mouth. My hands cupped her tits, squeezing until her nipples pebbled against my palms. She clawed at my hips, pulling me closer, grinding against my thigh.

Out of the corner of my eye, I saw him unzip, his cock already in his hand, stroking furiously.

Good boy.

We lowered ourselves onto the rug, spreading wide so he had the perfect view. Amira lay back, her legs open, her pussy glistening. I slid between her thighs, burying my tongue in her, licking, sucking, drinking her down as her cries echoed through the room.

Her hand tangled in my hair, pushing me deeper, her hips bucking. "Yes, Victoria, yes…"

I glanced up just long enough to see him groaning, his hand pumping harder, precum shining on his tip. His breathing was ragged, tortured, desperate.

Amira sat up suddenly, pulling me into her lap, flipping me onto my back. Her mouth devoured my cunt, her tongue circling my clit until I screamed. My nails raked the carpet, my back arched, and when I came, I came violently, gushing into her mouth as she lapped me up greedily.

The man moaned louder, his cock jerking in his fist, on the edge.

We didn't let him finish yet.

We turned together, crawling toward him, our mouths slick, our thighs shining, our pussies still trembling from orgasm. We spread ourselves open in front of him, side by side, touching each other while looking directly into his eyes.

"Come for us," I commanded.

Amira echoed, her voice dripping with hunger. "Yes. Show us."

That was it. His groan tore through the room, his body jerking as hot streams of cum shot across his stomach, spilling over his hand.

He collapsed back in the chair, spent, trembling.

We curled against each other on the rug, laughing wickedly, licking each other's mouths clean.

He was irrelevant. He'd been a spectator. A witness.

The real heat was between us.

✦ ✦ ✦

Chapter 24

Obedience

The thing about power is that once you've tasted it, once you've seen a man undone by nothing more than your rules, you want more.

Amira and I had agreed: this wasn't about falling into each other's arms. It wasn't about comfort or softness. It was about control. About the thrill of watching men stripped of theirs.

So our next game was simple.

We chose a man online. Professional, eager, polite in his messages — the kind who thought he was in control because he'd arranged the meeting. He had no idea what he was walking into.

When he arrived, I set the rules. Clear.

Uncompromising.

No touching, no speaking, no release unless commanded. Amira and I laid them out as soon as he walked through the door, and he nodded eagerly, already hard, already leaking in his trousers.

"Strip," Amira ordered.

He obeyed, fumbling out of his clothes until he stood naked in front of us, cock swollen and twitching.

We didn't touch him. Not at first.

We sprawled across the bed in our lingerie, kissing, teasing, tasting each other. His eyes devoured us while his cock jerked helplessly. Every moan from us dragged another groan from him.

"Stroke yourself," I commanded at last.

He obeyed instantly, pumping his cock, his body trembling with pent-up need.

But when his breathing quickened, I snapped, "Stop."

He froze, hand hovering, desperation written all over his face.

Amira smirked. "On your knees. Here."

He dropped to the floor beside the bed, cock bobbing, precum dripping onto his thigh. His eyes begged us, hungry and undone.

I slid down to the edge of the bed, Amira crawling beside me. We spread ourselves open for him, kissing each other while watching his restraint crumble. His cock jerked violently, desperate for release.

"Now," I whispered. "Come for us. Right here."

His groan shook the room as he pumped himself furiously, hot ropes of cum spurting across our thighs, our hands, our lingerie. He gasped, body convulsing, as we let it coat us, dripping down in messy, glorious streams.

Amira's eyes gleamed as she scooped it from her breast with two fingers and pushed them into my mouth. I sucked greedily, moaning as the salt filled my tongue.

Then I dipped my hand between his legs, collecting what was still dripping from his cock, and smeared it over Amira's lips. She licked them clean, her tongue darting to mine, and soon we were kissing, swapping his taste between us, devouring it like nectar.

He watched, destroyed, trembling as we consumed every drop of his orgasm, licking our fingers, our tits, each other, until there was nothing left but the sheen of sweat and the tang of victory.

We looked down at him — spent, panting, wide-eyed.

"You see?" I purred, stroking Amira's hair as she licked my fingers clean. "Your pleasure doesn't belong to you. It belongs to us."

And Amira laughed, low and wicked. "And we take all of it."

✦ ✦ ✦

Chapter 25
The Forbidden Show

It was Amira who confessed it.

We were lying naked in my bed, our skin still sticky with the last man's release we had devoured together, when she said it:

"There's someone at the café. A member. I've wanted him for years."

Her voice was hesitant, almost guilty. "He's quiet. Polished. Always sits in the same corner with a book. I've imagined… putting on a show for him. Letting him see me, really see me. But the rules…" She trailed off, biting her lip.

I propped myself up on one elbow, studying her. Amira, the gatekeeper of discretion, the one who had enforced silence with an iron brow, fantasising about tearing down her own walls. It was irresistible.

"The rules make it hotter," I said with a wicked smile. "And you know it."

She shivered.

"But we'd need absolute discretion," she whispered. "No one else could ever know. Not the other members. Not the staff. Him, me, and you. That's it."

"Strict boundaries," I agreed, stroking her hair. "Which makes it a perfect challenge."

It was Amira's stage now.

Everything about her was immaculate when she stepped onto the floor of Deep Blend. Her hair pinned, her blouse buttoned, her heels clicking in quiet rhythm across the polished wood. The perfect manager. The enforcer of rules.

But I knew what she'd put on underneath. No knickers. Black stockings. Suspender belt. Lace cut to tempt and taunt.

And I knew exactly who she was dressing for.

He was already there in his usual Thursday alcove chair, book in hand, coffee cooling untouched at his elbow. Always alone, always discreet. Dial always on red. He looked up briefly when she entered, then dropped his gaze as if nothing had stirred. But his grip on the book was tighter than usual.

Amira passed behind the partition, directly into his line of sight, but invisible to everyone else. She bent at the waist, fussing with the lampshade, her skirt lifting just enough to bare the lace tops of her stockings. No knickers, nothing underneath but glistening, waiting flesh.

His book stilled. His eyes widened, hungry, disbelieving.

And Amira gave him more.

She slid her hand behind her, fingers stroking her slit, slow and filthy, then brought them up to her mouth. She sucked them clean, lips closing around her own arousal, tongue flicking. All the while her face betrayed nothing to the rest of the café. Professional. Poised. Perfect.

But in his private view, she was pure sin.

I saw it from my table, feigning a novel in hand. The way his breathing changed. The way his thighs shifted. His free hand trembled as he held his book higher, hiding what he was doing underneath.

Amira leaned against the partition now, sliding two fingers inside herself, her head tilting back, her mouth opening in a soft, silent moan. She fucked herself slowly, shamelessly, her hips rocking just enough to make it clear what she was doing.

His hand moved faster beneath the book. His jaw clenched. His face flushed crimson with lust and shame.

Then Amira licked her fingers again, this time dripping wet, deliberately letting a strand of slick glisten between her lips and her hand. Her eyes found his over the partition. Locked. Held. Dared.

He broke.

The book trembled violently. His face twisted, his hips jerking as he yanked his rock hard cock free under its cover, stroking furiously now, no pretence left. His breath caught in ragged, silent gasps until his whole body tensed—

And then he spilled.

Hot ropes of cum spurted across the open pages of his book, splattering, soaking the neat print in filthy streaks. He froze, trembling, panting through clenched teeth, trying to smother the sounds of his release.

Amira, ever the professional, smoothed her skirt down, buttoned her blouse back up, and walked calmly to her desk without a trace of guilt on her face.

To anyone else, she was still the perfect guardian of Deep Blend.

But he knew. She knew. And I knew.

And the way her eyes met mine for just one fleeting second as she sat down told me everything:

Amira had discovered her power — and she was never going back.

✦ ✦ ✦

Chapter 26
The Confession

She came to me that night after work, still in her uniform, the faintest sheen of sweat on her forehead, her eyes too bright to be calm.

I poured her a drink, but she didn't touch it. She paced instead, hands trembling, her whole body humming with something she couldn't yet put into words.

Finally she stopped, turned, and blurted it out:

"Victora, that was the filthiest thing I've ever done."

Her voice cracked with both shock and hunger. "I touched myself at work. In uniform. Right behind the partition. He watched every second. He came all over his bloody book."

Her hands shook as she pressed them to her face, but she wasn't crying. She was laughing — wicked, disbelieving, exhilarated.

"I should feel ashamed," she said. "God, I should. But I don't. I can't. I've never felt so powerful in my life."

I smiled slowly, walking toward her, glass in hand. "Because you made him lose control. You took years of his composure and snapped it in ten minutes. That's not shame, Amira. That's power."

She shuddered, her breath catching.

"And now?" I asked softly, close enough that she could feel my breath against her ear.

"Now I want more," she whispered. "Bigger. Riskier. I want to see how far I can take it. I want to know how much I can make a man break before he explodes. And I want to do it again, Victora. Again and again."

Her eyes locked on mine, fever-bright, desperate. "Teach me. Show me how to push them. How to hold them on the edge until they beg."

I set down the untouched glass, sliding my hands over her shoulders, down to her waist. She trembled under my touch, not from fear but anticipation.

"Oh, darling," I murmured, my lips brushing hers, "you're not just my student anymore. You're becoming my partner. My equal."

Her smile was sharp, hungry. "Then let's hunt. But this time, I want him begging. I want him on his knees."

And I knew then that Amira wasn't just dipping her toes in the water anymore. She was diving headfirst into the filth, and I would be right beside her, pulling men down into the depths.

✦ ✦ ✦

Chapter 27

Addicted

Amira came to me shaking again — but this time it wasn't nerves. It was hunger.

She dropped onto my sofa, her uniform still neat, her blouse still buttoned, but her legs wouldn't stay still. Her thighs pressed together, then apart, her hands clenched, her breath uneven.

"Victora," she whispered, "I can't stop thinking about it. Him pulling his cock out right there in the café. Stroking himself, trying not to make a sound, and then… the mess on his book. That image won't leave me."

Her lips parted, her face flushed. "It made me feel… God, it made me feel like I was untouchable. Like I had him on a leash and he couldn't even breathe without my permission."

I smiled, slow and knowing. "And now you want it again."

Her eyes snapped to mine, wide and desperate. "Yes. I need it. I need another show, Victora. In public. Somewhere no one else notices. Just him and me. Just us breaking the rules while the world keeps spinning around us."

Her laugh was breathless, half-mad with need. "I don't even care if it's the same man. In fact—" she paused, biting her lip, "I want it to be. He knows what I can do now. I want to see how far I can push him. How quickly I can break him. How shameless I can make him."

I leaned closer, my hand sliding along her thigh, feeling the heat burning through her stockings. "Then we plan it properly. We make it filthier. Riskier. But still… invisible."

Her breath hitched. "Behind the partition again?"

"Somewhere even bolder," I murmured. "Close enough that anyone glancing might notice something… off. But subtle enough they won't know what."

She shivered, her thighs clenching tighter. "Victora, if I make him do it again — if I make him pull out his cock and cum in public, where anyone could see — I think I'll lose my mind."

I kissed her cheek, whispering into her ear: "Darling, that's not losing your mind. That's discovering it."

She trembled under my lips, her pulse racing.

And I knew then that Amira was fully gone — addicted to the rush, the taboo, the thrill of turning the quietest corner of her world into her personal stage for sin.

This wasn't about men anymore. It wasn't about sex.

It was about power.

And Amira wanted it dripping from every forbidden
place she could claim.

✦ ✦ ✦

Chapter 28
The Next Stage

The café man had been her proof.

She'd whispered it to me, almost giddy with pride: "Victora, do you know what it means? If you can make a man so desperate he takes his cock out in public and cums in front of you? That's real power."

And she was right. She had him wrapped. She could have played with him forever. But Amira was greedy now. She didn't just want one man under her spell. She wanted more. New prey. A bigger audience, even if it was only one set of eyes.

So she chose her stage carefully.

A train. Evening service. Packed enough that no one paid attention to anyone else, but quiet enough in certain carriages to carve out a little island of secrecy.

That was where she found him — a businessman, late fifties, tie loosened, laptop bag at his feet, scrolling through his phone with weary detachment. The type of man who thought he was invisible.

Amira slid into the seat opposite him, crossing her legs slowly, deliberately. To anyone else, it was nothing. To him, it was a flash of lace beneath her uniform skirt. His eyes flicked down, then away, embarrassed — but she caught it. She always caught it.

She leaned back, feigning boredom, her hand drifting to her throat, tracing her collarbone, then lower, the swell of her breasts just visible as she tugged her blouse an inch wider.

His phone froze in his hand.

The train hummed on. Passengers around them shifted, read newspapers, dozed. No one noticed the silent theatre unfolding between Amira and her target.

She let her fingers trail down to her thigh, just under the hem of her skirt. She parted her legs slightly, enough for him to see the dark wetness staining her lace. Then she slid two fingers inside herself, slow and obscene, never breaking eye contact with him.

His breath caught audibly.

He tried to look away. He couldn't. His hand shifted in his lap, fumbling, hesitant. She licked her fingers, deliberately sucking them one by one, her tongue glistening, her lips wrapping around her own arousal.

And that was it.

His shame crumbled. His hand unzipped with a shaky urgency, his cock emerging under the table, shielded only by the thin edge of his laptop bag. His strokes were fast, desperate, his eyes locked on her as if hypnotised.

Amira leaned forward, whispering without sound, her lips shaping the word "come."

He obeyed.

His jaw clenched, his body jerking as hot streams of cum spilled across his shirt and bag, staining his suit trousers, soaking into the fabric with filthy finality.

He froze in horror, breath ragged, fumbling to cover the mess, his cheeks crimson with shame.

And Amira?

She smoothed her skirt, buttoned her blouse, and sat back as if nothing had happened. A queen among pawns.

When she stepped off the train two stops later, her face was composed, her stride unhurried. But when she spotted me waiting on the platform, her lips curved into the smallest, most wicked smile.

"I did it," she whispered in my ear as we walked away. "And Victora — it was even easier this time."

✦ ✦ ✦

Chapter 29
Her Turn

The shift was subtle at first.

Amira still talked about control, about making men crumble, but there was a new heat in her eyes whenever she replayed the details. The café man's book, the businessman's trousers, the stain of their shame.

But then she admitted it one night, her cheeks flushed, her thighs pressed tight together.

"Victora… it's not enough just watching them. I want the rush myself. I want to feel what it's like to touch myself in public. To come where anyone could see me. I want the risk. The filth. The thrill of knowing someone's watching and can't stop me."

I leaned in, kissed her ear. "Then we'll make it happen."

We chose a late-night bar — dim lighting, low music, booths tucked into corners. The kind of place where people mind their own business.

Amira wore her uniform blouse with nothing underneath. She slid into the booth opposite me, her skirt hitched high enough that her bare thighs gleamed in the soft light.

She ordered a drink, calm, poised, the perfect manager out for an evening. Then, once the waiter was gone, she leaned back, spread her legs, and slid her hand beneath the table.

Her eyes locked on mine.

The first moan was soft, controlled, but her fingers were already glistening when she brought them up to her mouth, sucking them clean right there in the bar.

No one noticed — except one.

A man two tables over. His eyes widened, then darted away. But he kept glancing back, restless, unable to help himself.

Amira smirked, spreading her legs wider, stroking herself openly now, her breath coming quicker. I reached across, stroking her wrist, guiding her fingers faster.

And then she whispered, "I want more. I want him."

Before I could answer, she slid out of the booth, heels clicking, crossing the floor with a predator's grace. She stopped at his table, leaned down, whispered something in his ear. His face went scarlet, but he followed her without hesitation.

I gave them a minute, then pushed the door open to the alley beside the bar.

There she was — on her knees, skirt rucked up, blouse gaping, her lips stretched around his cock as she sucked him hard, shameless, moaning as though the whole world could hear.

He groaned, clutching the wall, hips bucking, trying to stifle the sounds. But Amira didn't let up. She sucked harder, deeper, one hand stroking herself furiously as she pushed him closer and closer.

When he came, it was violent, hot streams filling her mouth as she swallowed greedily, licking him clean before wiping her lips with the back of her hand.

And then she came too — a cry muffled against his thigh, her body shuddering as her orgasm ripped through her, wetness dripping down her thighs into her stockings.

She stood, composed her blouse, smoothed her hair, and walked back toward me with a wicked smile.

Her voice was hoarse when she leaned in close. "Victora, I don't just like the power anymore. I like the dirt. The risk. The shame. And I want it again."

✦ ✦ ✦

Chapter 30
Indulgence

I'd always told myself I was the teacher, the steady hand guiding Amira through her descent into filth. But the truth? Watching her spiral deeper into the taboo, I was burning right alongside her.

She was addicted. And now, so was I.

That night, when she whispered, "Victora, I don't just want one. I want more. Three. At once. You and me together." — something inside me snapped. I didn't hesitate.

We chose them recklessly. Two from the bar, one from the alley — men who couldn't take their eyes off us. Hungry, eager, stupid enough to follow.

When the flat door clicked shut, it was like unleashing a storm.

"Stop." I held up a hand before they could lunge. My voice was sharp, commanding. "You don't touch us yet. You watch. And you stroke."

Amira grinned at me, eyes gleaming. She pulled her blouse open, slow, teasing, letting her tits spill free. I stripped my dress away, stockings still on, heels still strapped. We climbed onto the sofa together, curling into each other, our bodies pressed, our lips meeting in a long, wet kiss.

The men groaned already, cocks out, pumping in their fists, their eyes devouring us.

We put on the show.

Amira spread her legs wide, sliding her fingers over her dripping slit, moaning as I bent to suck her nipples, my tongue circling until she gasped. I licked down her belly, teasing, stroking myself as the three men stroked harder, their knuckles white, their cocks slick with precum.

"Faster," I ordered, glancing at them. "Show us how badly you want it."

Their breathing grew ragged. Their bodies shook.

Amira sucked my fingers, then slid them back inside her cunt, her eyes fluttering. I straddled her thigh, grinding shamelessly, my clit throbbing against her skin. We kissed again, tongues slick, our moans deliberately loud.

The men were wrecked already. Their hands blurred, their cocks glistening, heavy, swollen. One groaned so loudly he clamped his fist over his mouth.

I pulled back, licking Amira's juices from my fingers. "Don't you dare come yet," I told them. "If you do, you're out."

They froze, trembling, their desperation almost laughable.

Amira looked at me, eyes wild, and whispered, "Victora, let's take them."

I smiled wickedly. "Yes. Let's use them."

Amira dropped to her knees first, taking one in her mouth, stroking another with her hand, moaning as though she was starving. I grabbed the third, guiding him against my lips, sucking him deep while another's hand tangled in my hair.

The room was filled with groans, gasps, wet sounds. Filth.

"Swap," I commanded, pulling Amira's hair back. Our mouths changed cocks, messy, dripping, strings of spit falling to our tits as we gagged and swallowed them down.

They fucked our mouths like they owned us, but it was the opposite — we had them, all three, trembling, desperate, powerless against our hunger.

I climbed onto the sofa, spreading wide as one man slid into me hard, relentless, pounding until the wet smacks filled the room. Beside me, Amira was bent over, moaning as another filled her from behind while she sucked the third, gagging, drooling, swallowing every inch.

It was obscene. Unmerciful. A blur of cocks and mouths and wetness, every hole filled, every cry louder, every thrust deeper.

Amira screamed as she came, squirting across the floor, soaking the man inside her as he roared his climax. I came seconds later, my pussy clenching around thick heat as another spilled inside me.

And the third? He jerked over us both, hot ropes of cum striping our tits, our faces, dripping from our mouths as we licked each other clean, laughing like sinners who'd burned the rulebook.

We collapsed in a heap, tangled in sweat and semen, the men groaning, spent, used.

Amira turned to me, her face shining, her chest heaving. "Victora… this is it. This is everything I wanted."

And the truth was, I wanted it just as badly.

✦ ✦ ✦

Chapter 31
The Word Spreads

The whispers had become impossible to ignore. Amira's "partition show" hadn't stayed secret — of course it hadn't. Men are terrible at keeping their lust contained.

But instead of disgust or reprisal, the request came.

"After closing. No outsiders. No staff. Just us. We want to see for ourselves."

Twelve men. Twelve members. Each polished, professional, immaculate in the daylight — now sitting in silence across the leather armchairs and dark wood paneling, their eyes locked on us with hunger that stripped away every layer of civility.

Amira and I stood in the centre of the café, the lamplight dim, the hush thicker than ever.

"This is madness," she whispered in my ear. But her body betrayed her — trembling, flushed, wet already under her uniform.

I kissed her neck. "It's power, Amira. And tonight, we own them all."

She began first — unbuttoning her blouse, slowly, teasingly, letting each clasp fall until her breasts spilled free, nipples stiff, aching under their gaze. A ripple went through the room, the men shifting, throats clearing, trousers tightening.

I dropped to my knees, sliding her skirt up, parting her thighs wide to show the glossy wet lace beneath. Then I licked her, long and filthy, moaning against her cunt as the men groaned.

"Cocks out," I commanded. My voice was sharp, absolute.

The rustle was immediate. Zippers rasped, belts clattered, trousers fell. Twelve cocks sprang free, thick, heavy, leaking with desperation.

And that's when the frenzy began.

We didn't divide them neatly. We let them swarm.

One shoved his cock between my tits as I squeezed them tight around him, licking the tip with each thrust. Another filled Amira's mouth, groaning as she gagged and drooled, her lips stretched wide. Two knelt behind us, sliding into our pussies hard, relentless, their hips smacking against our soaked thighs.

I screamed into Amira's cunt as I licked her, another cock pressed to my lips, shoving deep until I choked on his salt. She moaned around her mouthful, her eyes watering as another man gripped her hair and fucked her throat raw.

It was chaos. Flesh slapping, moans echoing, cocks pounding every hole they could take.

I bent forward, sucking one cock while jerking another, hot streams spurting over my face as he came, dripping into my mouth, onto my tits. Amira straddled one man, riding him hard, while two others stroked themselves over her breasts, groaning as they covered her chest in sticky cum.

"Don't stop," I gasped, my body quaking as another man spilled inside me, hot cum flooding my cunt until it leaked down my thighs. "Use us. All of you."

They obeyed like animals.

Twelve men, spilling one after another. On our faces. In our mouths. Across our tits. Inside our pussies until we dripped with their seed. They came at different intervals, wave after wave, until the floor, the chairs, even the air smelled thick with sex.

Amira knelt beside me, panting, her hair wild, her skin glazed in semen. I grabbed her, kissed her deep, both of us licking cum from each other's mouths as the last of them groaned his cum over our joined tongues.

When it was done, we collapsed together in the centre of the café, drenched, shaking, our bodies painted with filth.

The men sat ruined, their cocks soft, their faces slack with shock and pleasure.

Amira's voice was hoarse, but her eyes gleamed. "Victora… we've turned Deep Blend into a brothel of our own making."

I licked a strand of cum from her cheek and whispered back:

"No, darling. We've turned it into our kingdom."

◆ ◆ ◆

Chapter 32
Aftermath

The morning after, the flat reeked of cum.

Our bodies ached. My thighs were bruised, my tits tender, my throat raw from cocks that had fucked me until I gagged. Amira stirred beside me, her hair tangled, her skin sticky in patches where dried cum clung stubbornly even after a shower.

We lay in silence for a while, the events of the night flooding back in jagged waves. Twelve men. Hands everywhere. Mouths, cocks, hot ropes of seed painting us until we were soaked and laughing, kissing through the filth.

Amira finally broke the quiet, her voice hoarse.

"Victora… that was the dirtiest, most dangerous thing I've ever done."

Her lips curled into a wicked smile. "And I've never felt more alive."

I rolled onto my side, stroking her hip, tasting the faint salt still clinging to her skin. "We made them animals. We turned twelve civilised men into begging, spurting wrecks."

She laughed softly, but the sound faltered. Her eyes darkened. "I'm the manager, Victoria. Do you understand what that means? If this ever gets out… I don't just lose the café. I lose everything. My reputation. My livelihood."

I brushed her cheek with my thumb. "They won't breathe a word."

Her brow furrowed. "How can you be so sure?"

"Because they'd ruin themselves too," I said. "Every one of them. It wasn't just you and me breaking the rules last night — it was all of them. The very men who built their lives on discretion and restraint. If they talk, they burn. And they know it."

She let out a shaky laugh. "So we're safe because they're guilty too."

"Exactly," I purred. "Our little kingdom of filth survives because no one can afford to admit it exists."

Amira closed her eyes, her hand sliding between her thighs almost unconsciously. 'God, Victora… even now I'm still wet. Just remembering them, all of them, spilling over us…' She moaned softly, her hips rolling. "It wasn't just sex. It was power. It was being worshipped in the filthiest way."

I leaned down, licking her fingers as she touched herself. "And it won't be the last time."

Her eyes snapped open, hungry again despite the bruises, despite the danger.

"Promise me that," she whispered. "Promise me we'll do it again."

I kissed her deep, tasting her arousal, tasting the ghost of last night still on her lips.

"Darling," I murmured, "this is only the beginning."

✦ ✦ ✦

Chapter 33
Daylight Games

It was almost funny.

By day, Deep Blend looked unchanged. The same soft lamplight. The same hush of pages turning. The same scent of coffee and polish. Members drifting in and out with their quiet airs of civility.

But I knew. And Amira knew. And most of all — they knew.

The twelve who'd stayed late, who'd seen us drenched in cum, who'd spilled themselves over our tits, in our mouths, across the polished floor — they were sitting here now, scattered among the others, playing their roles as if nothing had ever happened.

But their eyes betrayed them.

A glance too long. A twitch of a jaw. The memory flashing hot behind their masks of restraint.

Amira and I didn't need to speak. We'd planned it with the smallest gestures.

That day, she wore her uniform as always — crisp blouse, fitted skirt — but I knew what was underneath. Stockings. Lace. Nothing else. She passed between the chairs, collecting empty cups, straightening a magazine. Harmless to anyone else. But to those twelve, every movement was a performance. She bent at the waist to pick up a stray napkin, skirt lifting just enough to show the lace tops. I watched their throats tighten. Their hands shift against their trousers.

She stopped by one of them — a tall, broad man who always pretended to be buried in his books. His eyes flicked up when she passed, then down again as if ashamed of what he'd seen last time.

Amira lingered at his table a moment longer than necessary, rearranging a stack of journals. When she looked at him again, she gave the smallest, wickedest wink.

And mouthed the word: now.

I nearly laughed.

He froze, stunned, his hand twitching at his lap. His face flushed crimson, but slowly, carefully, his book shifted higher, just enough to shield his lap from anyone else. His hand slipped beneath the table.

I saw it. Amira saw it. His knuckles tightening, his jaw clenched, the unmistakable rhythm of a man stroking himself in public silence.

Amira straightened, her face composed, her tone polite as she murmured, "Everything to your liking, sir?"

The irony nearly undid me.

He nodded stiffly, breath uneven, his hand still moving under the table. His cock must have been aching, swelling against his palm.

Amira walked away, her hips swaying deliberately. But as she passed me, her eyes gleamed.

I joined in. Shifting in my seat, I slid my skirt higher, spreading my thighs just enough that the man could glimpse lace and wetness glistening. I traced circles over my clit, book balanced in one hand, my breath shallow but quiet.

His face contorted. His hand moved faster. His body trembled.

I knew he was close.

And then Amira glanced back over her shoulder, lips parting in a mock gasp as if she felt his climax. That was all it took.

His hips jerked under the table. His mouth opened in a silent groan. And then the telltale shudder, the brief freeze, the sag of release. He came right there in the middle of Deep Blend, spurting hot cum against his trousers, cum spilling into his palm, soaking the cloth beneath his book.

No one else noticed. Not a page stopped turning. Not a cup stopped clinking.

But Amira and I knew. We'd made him do it. And that power thrummed in my veins like fire.

Amira walked calmly back to the counter, smoothing her skirt, tucking a strand of hair behind her ear as if nothing had happened.

Her lips barely moved when she caught my eye across the room.

'One down. Eleven to go.'

Chapter 34
The Proposition

The whispers never stopped.

No matter how discreet we tried to be, the after-hours orgy had planted roots in every corner of the membership. They wanted more. Some begged with their eyes. Others with discreet notes. The ones who'd been there wanted it repeated. The ones who hadn't wanted in.

But then came something different. Something far more dangerous.

He was one of the wealthier members. You could tell by the cut of his suits, the polished cufflinks, the quiet arrogance of a man who'd never been denied anything in his life. He lingered after hours one evening, when the last cup had been cleared and the blinds were drawn.

"Ladies," he said smoothly, his voice calm, confident. "We need to talk."

Amira stiffened. For a moment, I thought this was it — discovery, exposure, the ruin of everything. But then he smiled. Not cruelly. Not threateningly. Almost conspiratorial.

"What you've created here," he continued, "is extraordinary. A sanctuary by day. A... playground by night. I've never seen anything like it."

He paused, watching our faces carefully. "And I think it should spread."

Amira blinked. "Spread?"

"Franchises," he said simply. "London doesn't have to be the only one. We could establish Deep Blend in other cities. Edinburgh. Manchester. Bristol. Quiet, discreet, members-only cafés by day. And at night…" His smile widened. "…the same indulgences you've already proven possible here."

My heart hammered.

"You want to make this… bigger?" I asked slowly.

He nodded. "The demand is there. Believe me. And I have the money, the network, the reach. But what I don't have—" he looked directly at us, eyes sharp with hunger— "is you. The heart of it. The ones who make the fantasy real."

Amira's face was unreadable, but I knew her well enough to see the flicker in her eyes. Fear. Excitement. Lust.

A network of Deep Blend. More cities. More men. More shows. More filth.

But also more risk. Exposure. Danger.

Amira licked her lips, her voice low. "And what would you expect from us?"

He leaned back, utterly at ease. "Exactly what you've already done. To teach. To lead. To be the centrepiece. Every man who walks through the doors would know he's in the presence of women who can undo him without a word."

I felt my cunt throb at the thought. Power, spread across an entire country.

But I also felt the weight of the noose tightening around our necks.

Amira caught my hand under the table. Her grip was trembling. Her voice, when it came, was almost a whisper.

"Victora… what if this is our destiny?"

He leaned forward, resting his elbows on the polished table, cufflinks flashing under the lamp.

"Let me be clear," he said smoothly. "This isn't about simply opening coffee shops. It's about creating a network. A chain of sanctuaries where the lonely, the hungry, the frustrated can come under the guise of civility… but those who know, those willing to pay the price, can access something far more carnal.

"And at the heart of each? Women like you."

Amira's breath caught. "Women like us?"

"Yes," he said. "Mentors. Performers. Guides. Not whores, not escorts — but queens. The ones who bend men without touching them. Who command obedience in silence. Who take power in ways no money can buy."

He paused, letting it sink in.

"You wouldn't be alone. You'd select and train others — the right women. Discreet, sharp, beautiful in spirit as well as flesh. Women who can follow your lead, who understand this isn't about sex alone. It's about power. About creating the 'Deep Blend signature.'

My cunt pulsed at his words. A signature. As if Amira and I had invented something that could be bottled and exported.

Amira leaned back, her voice low, cautious but trembling with excitement. "And you think there are other women who would do this?"

He smiled knowingly. "Victoria, Amira… you'd be surprised how many women ache to wield power but don't know how. You've discovered something rare. I'm offering you the chance to cultivate it."

He produced a leather folder, sliding it across the table. Inside were figures, maps, names of possible locations. Manchester. Bristol. Edinburgh. A spread of discreet addresses, wealthy neighbourhoods, all ripe for this twisted expansion.

"And of course," he added softly, "you'd be compensated. Handsomely. Not just money. Influence. Protection. Men who'd never dare betray you because they'd have more to lose than you ever would."

Amira stared at the folder, her fingers trembling as she touched the edge. Her eyes flicked to mine, wide and conflicted.

"What if it all comes crashing down?" she whispered.

He chuckled. "Then it crashes on my head, not yours. I'll be the financier. The face. You two? You'll be the spirit, the untouchable flame. No one ever sees the firekeepers. They only feel the heat."

Amira and I sat in silence, staring at one another.

I could see it in her eyes. The fear. The danger. The thrill.

And I knew she could see the same in mine.

✦ ✦ ✦

Chapter 35

The Plan

We didn't answer him immediately. We couldn't.

The folder sat heavy on Amira's desk long after he'd gone, pages of figures and maps peeking out like a promise — or a threat.

That night, we poured wine and curled on my sofa, both of us restless, both of us aroused by something far bigger than lust.

"So," I said, twirling the stem of my glass. "Franchises. Edinburgh. Manchester. Us… mentors."

Amira laughed, though her voice shook. "Victora, it sounds insane. We're café girls turned queens of filth, and now someone wants to make us… a brand."

I smirked. "Deep Blend™. Our own filthy empire."

But then her face grew serious. "Could we even do it? Find the right women? Teach them how to move, how to control men without a word?"

I set down my glass and slid closer, running a hand up her thigh. "We'd teach them the same way I taught you.

Gesture. Presence. Power in silence. And of course…"
I let my hand slip higher, brushing her lace"…practice."

Her breath caught.

I reached for the toy box I'd placed beside the sofa
earlier, laying it open like a velvet invitation: straps,
plugs, wands, sleek silicone shapes glinting in the
lamplight.

Amira's lips parted. "So we'd… what? Break them in
gently?"

I picked up the wand, flicked it on, the hum filling the
room like a secret engine. Pressing it against her thigh, I
teased her, my own cunt already clenching in
anticipation. "Not gently. Thoroughly. Make them feel
what power tastes like. Let them drown in it until it's
second nature."

She moaned, hips lifting as I slid the wand against her
soaked pussy. Her hands clawed at the cushions, her
eyes rolling back as waves of vibration shook her.

I straddled her, grinding against her stomach, the hum
of the wand resonating through both our bodies.

"And what about us?" she gasped.

I pushed her back further, kissing down her chest,
sucking her nipples while the wand pulsed mercilessly at

her cunt. She came suddenly, squirting violently, her thighs clamping around my wrist as her juices spilled over my hand.

But I wasn't finished.

Before she could recover, I pulled the wand away, slick and shining, and pressed it hard against my own pussy. The jolt made me cry out, my hips bucking uncontrollably.

Amira's hand shot out, fingers sinking into me, curling, stroking in rhythm with the wand. "Come for me, Clara," she whispered hoarsely. "Show me how we'll teach them. Show me how shameless we'll be."

The words undid me. My orgasm ripped through me like fire, soaking her hand, my body shuddering, convulsing against her.

When it passed, we lay side by side, panting, slick with sweat and arousal, the toy box still open beside us.

I turned my head, kissed her, tasting both of us on her lips.

"See?" I murmured. "Training isn't theory. It's practice. And we'll practice until we're unstoppable."

She laughed weakly, stroking my cheek. "Then we'll need more toys."

We both burst out laughing, our bodies tangled, our minds spinning not just with lust but with the dizzying prospect of what was to come: an empire of filth, and us as its queens.

✦ ✦ ✦

Chapter 36

The Manchester Experiment

The hotel suite felt more like a theatre than a room.

The curtains were drawn, the lamps turned low. Four women sat in a line — Sophie, Maya, Helen, Alina — watching with wide eyes. Tonight wasn't theirs. Tonight was ours. Their only task was to see and understand.

Amira and I were the lesson.

Six men sat across from us in leather chairs, silent, cocks hidden for now. They were our instruments.

"Rule one," I told the women, pacing before them. "You don't perform for men. You torment them. Every gasp, every ache, every twitch of their cocks is yours to control. You let them suffer. You keep them aching."

Amira smiled, unclasping her blouse slowly, one button at a time. "If they're desperate enough, they'll come without touch. That's when you know you have them."

We began.

I slid onto the bed, legs spread, the wand humming against my clit. Amira knelt between my thighs, licking, sucking, moaning. My back arched, my cries filled the room, but I kept one eye on the men — watching their jaws clench, their fists twitching, their cocks swelling under their trousers.

"Not yet," I said sharply. "You don't touch yourselves until we allow it."

The women glanced at me, startled. They hadn't realised it could be that strict.

Amira licked her way up my stomach, kissing my breasts, biting my nipples until I screamed. My wand thrummed harder, my thighs shaking. The men groaned, shifting in their chairs, desperate for release.

One moaned aloud, a sound of pure agony. His cock was so hard it strained against the fabric. His face twisted as his hips jerked, and suddenly he spurted hot cum into his trousers — untouched.

The women gasped.

I smiled darkly. "See? The best performers never even need a cock in their hands. You control them so completely their bodies betray them."

Amira climbed onto my face, riding my tongue while I shoved the wand between her thighs. Her moans turned to cries, filthy and raw, filling the room like music.

The men squirmed, eyes glazed, cocks throbbing.

I lifted my head, voice sharp. "Cocks out. But don't stroke."

They obeyed instantly — five thick, leaking cocks jutting into the air, purple with frustration, desperate for touch.

The women stared, transfixed. Sophie bit her lip so hard it nearly bled. Maya whispered 'oh my god.' Helen's chest rose and fell in frantic bursts. Alina…

she still sat still, but her thighs pressed tightly together.

Amira ground against my tongue, her body shaking, juices spilling over my mouth. The men groaned, fists clenching at their sides.

"Hold," I barked. "You don't touch until we say."

And then it happened again — another man, trembling, gasping, his cock jerking violently as cum sprayed across his stomach and thighs, untouched. The women stared in shock.

Amira pulled off me, her face wet, her cunt glistening. She turned to them, panting.

"This is what you aim for. Not just stroking men off. Not just sucking them dry. But breaking them with your show, holding them in agony until they erupt on their own. That's power. That's the Deep Blend signature."

By the time we allowed the rest to wank, the men were so desperate they came within seconds, spurting cum over their hands, their bellies, their shoes, groaning like animals.

The women sat silent, faces flushed, thighs clenched, their eyes wide with the hunger of understanding.

"Tomorrow," I told them softly, "it will be you keeping them on the edge. And when you hold a man in such agony he comes without your touch…"

I licked Amira's juices from my lips, smirking.

"…that's when you'll know you're ready."

✦ ✦ ✦

Chapter 37

Sophie and Alina's Lesson

The men returned the next night. Six of them again, restless, hard before they'd even sat down. They wanted release, but more than that, they wanted the show.

Tonight, it was Sophie and Alina's turn.

Sophie looked almost feral — cheeks flushed, lips bitten raw, desperate to prove herself. Alina stood beside her, calm, composed, a mask of ice hiding whatever storm lay beneath.

"Together," I told them, stepping back. "Deep Blend isn't about solo acts. It's about women feeding off one another. The tease is stronger when it comes from two mouths, two bodies, two sets of eyes."

Amira circled them, her voice low, instructive. "One drives the fire, the other controls the heat. Sophie — you'll be the spark. Alina — you'll be the silence that unnerves them."

The women nodded, eyes locked forward.

Sophie was the first to move. She peeled her dress down, revealing her tits, full and heavy in black lace.

She squeezed them together, moaning, licking her own cleavage before turning to Alina.

"Touch me," she whispered.

For a moment I thought Alina would refuse. But then, slowly, deliberately, she reached out and cupped Sophie's breast, thumb circling her nipple. Sophie gasped loudly, arching her back. The men groaned.

I snapped my fingers sharply. "Cocks out."

The sound of zips and belts filled the room. Six cocks jutted into the air, thick, leaking. Their hands hovered, trembling.

"Don't stroke," Amira commanded. "Not until they tell you."

Alina dropped to her knees suddenly, pulling Sophie's lace panties down and pressing her mouth against her cunt. The quiet one transformed, eating her with slow, obscene licks, moaning softly as Sophie cried out above her.

The men squirmed in their seats, fists clenching, thighs trembling.

Sophie tangled her fingers in Alina's hair, grinding against her tongue, her tits bouncing with each gasp. She turned to the men, her voice trembling but firm.

"Not yet. You'll wait."

The command landed. The men groaned in agony, their cocks twitching violently, balls drawn up tight, desperate for release.

I guided them further. "Now make them believe you'll finish… but don't."

Alina pulled away, her lips glistening, and kissed Sophie deeply, their tongues tangling, Sophie's juices shining between them. They moaned into each other's mouths, grinding together, the sounds wet and obscene.

One man whimpered — 'please.' His cock jerked violently, spraying hot cum across his lap without a touch.

The other women gasped. Sophie froze, shocked, then laughed breathlessly.

"That," I told her, my voice sharp, "is the signature. Two women performing. Men aching, spilling without permission. That is when you know you own them."

Amira stepped forward, her eyes flashing. "Now you may release them."

Sophie smirked, licking Alina's lips clean, then turned to the men. "Stroke."

The room filled with groans as five fists pumped desperately, cum spurting across bellies and thighs in seconds. They collapsed back, ruined.

Sophie and Alina stood panting, their faces shining, their bodies wet. Sophie looked triumphant. Alina's mask cracked for the first time, her lips curved into the faintest, wickedest smile.

They were learning.

They were becoming us.

✦ ✦ ✦

Chapter 38

Maya and Helen's Lesson

By the third evening, the air in the suite had shifted.

The men had learned to expect torment. Their cocks twitched at the mere sight of the drawn curtains, the velvet chairs lined up facing the centre of the room. They knew the game now: they would be made to suffer, to ache, to writhe, until one by one their control snapped.

Tonight, the tormentors were Maya and Helen.

Maya was jittery, bouncing on her heels, eager to shock. Helen, in contrast, looked carved from marble: elegant blouse, pencil skirt, hair still immaculate. But I could see the flush on her throat, the rise and fall of her chest.

Amira addressed them both. "Tonight, your task isn't simply to make men come. It's to stop them from coming. To drag them through the fire until they break without your permission."

I opened the toy box on the low table: wands, plugs, glass dildos gleaming in the light.

"Use these," I told them. "Not on the men. On each other. Make them ache for every sound, every shudder, but don't give them the release they crave until you're ready."

The six men sat down, silent, cocks already swelling under their trousers.

Maya was the first to move. She pulled off her dress in one motion, revealing her tight body in nothing but stockings. She grabbed a vibrator, flicked it on, and pressed it against Helen's thigh.

Helen gasped, startled, but quickly steadied herself. She removed her blouse slowly, deliberately, exposing the lace beneath, her nipples straining against the fabric. She took the vibrator from Maya, pressed it hard against her cunt, and growled softly.

The men groaned in unison, their hands twitching toward their zips.

Maya turned on them, grinning wickedly. "Not yet. Cocks out. But no touching."

The rustle filled the room again. Six thick, leaking cocks sprang free, pulsing with need.

Helen licked Maya's nipple, slow and deliberate, moaning against her skin. Maya squealed and bucked, grinding against Helen's thigh. The sound alone had the men shuddering, their cocks jerking.

"Hold them," I snapped. "Make them wait."

The two women tangled together on the bed, one riding the vibrator, the other sucking greedily at her breasts. They moaned, gasped, writhed, their pleasure deliberately loud, deliberately filthy.

The men squirmed, fists clenched, thighs trembling. One was on the brink, his cock jerking violently, but Helen caught him with a single sharp glance.

"Don't you dare," she said, her voice low and commanding.

He froze, his entire body trembling with the effort of denial.

Amira smirked. "Good. That's control."

Minutes passed. The room filled with the hum of toys, the wet sounds of tongues, the cries of women locked in their own storm. The men were shaking now, sweat pouring down their faces, their cocks purple, desperate.

Maya licked her fingers, moaning, her eyes locked on them as she slid her slick hand between Helen's thighs. Helen's composure cracked at last — she cried out, arching, trembling on the edge of climax. The sight broke two men. They erupted untouched, cum spilling across their laps, their groans muffled against clenched teeth.

The others held on, panting, their bodies screaming.

Helen shoved the vibrator deeper into Maya's cunt, making her scream, squirting cum across the bed, making the men jolt in their seats. One more lost his battle, cum shooting over his chest with a helpless moan.

Three down. Three still straining.

Amira nodded approvingly. "Better. Much better. The longer you hold them, the more they'll break for you. The more they'll need you."

Finally, Helen gave the signal. "Stroke."

The remaining three men groaned in relief, fists pumping furiously, their cum spurting in frantic bursts within seconds.

When it was done, Maya collapsed against Helen, both of them flushed, trembling, their thighs wet and glistening.

I stepped forward, cupping Maya's chin, forcing her eyes to meet mine.

"You see now?" I said softly. "You don't win by making men come. You win by keeping them desperate until their own bodies betray them."

Helen nodded, breathless, her lips curling into a slow smile. Maya grinned wildly, her eyes still burning.

They were learning. They were becoming dangerous.

And for the first time, I thought: soon, they might not even need us.

✦ ✦ ✦

Chapter 39

The Final Lesson

The suite had never felt so heavy.

Tonight was different. Tonight wasn't about denial, or torment, or holding men back until they came untouched. Tonight was about letting go. About the other side of the game.

The four women — Sophie, Maya, Helen, Alina — stood before the six men, naked now, their bodies flushed, their eyes sharp with a hunger I'd seen grow night after night.

Amira stepped forward, her voice calm but firm. "You've learned how to break men with your show. Now you'll learn how to let them use you. Tonight, you're not queens. You're toys. Sex dolls for their cocks. But—" she raised a finger, her eyes glinting— "you still perform. You give yourself to them for the spectacle. Not for their pleasure. For 'control through surrender.'

The women nodded, some trembling, some grinning.

I looked at them all and smiled. "Time to graduate."

It started with Sophie. She dropped to her knees before one man, taking his cock deep into her mouth, gagging, drool running down her chin. The others gasped — but her eyes flicked to them, daring them to follow.

Maya laughed breathlessly and climbed onto another man's lap, sinking down onto his cock with a squeal. She rode him wildly, tits bouncing, his groans filling the room.

Helen stroked two cocks at once, her face set in concentration, her professional poise stripped away, replaced with raw hunger. Alina — quiet, unreadable Alina — bent over the table, spreading herself wide, letting a man take her from behind. Her moans were low, guttural, each thrust making her hair whip across her face.

The men groaned, groaned, fucked, stroked, spilled. The air was thick with sweat, with the slap of flesh, the wet suck of mouths, the cries of women giving themselves up like dolls.

But it wasn't chaos. It was performance.

Every cry was louder than it needed to be, every moan a deliberate echo. Sophie gagged on cock until cum sprayed across her face, then she licked her lips and winked at the others. Helen pumped two men until they spurted over her tits, then smeared it across her nipples proudly.

Maya screamed as she rode harder, the man beneath her groaning, bucking, until he filled her cunt with hot cum that dripped down her thighs.

Alina was the last to break, shuddering as she was pounded from behind, her moans turning to guttural cries as cum spilled inside her. She collapsed forward, trembling, hair plastered to her face, a faint smile finally cracking her mask.

By the end, the room was wrecked — bodies collapsed in chairs, cum streaking thighs, bellies, faces. The women lay sprawled across the carpet and bed, panting, dripping, ruined but radiant.

Amira and I stood at the edge, watching.

"They're ready," she said quietly.

I nodded. "They're Deep Blend now."

Sophie laughed breathlessly, wiping cum from her cheek. Maya collapsed against Helen, still giggling. Alina raised her head slowly, her eyes calm, her lips curved into the faintest, knowing smile. The training was over.

The show had begun.

Chapter 40

The Debut

The Manchester café was transformed after dark.

The lamps were dimmed, the shelves draped in velvet, the leather chairs set out in a half-circle facing the performance floor. A dozen men sat waiting, all high-paying members, chosen carefully. Their cocks twitched beneath their trousers, but not one of them dared move.

They knew this was history. The first Deep Blend performance outside London.

And the show belonged to Sophie, Maya, Helen, and Alina.

The four women entered together. Naked for only stockings and suspenders. Gleaming. Their bodies oiled, their eyes bright with hunger.

They didn't look at the men. Not yet.

Instead, they fell on each other.

Sophie pressed Maya down onto the rug, sliding two fingers into her cunt while sucking her tits. Helen straddled Alina's face, grinding against her mouth while toying with her own clit. The air filled with moans, wet sounds, the hum of toys.

The men groaned, fists twitching, but no one moved.

I leaned against the back wall with Amira, smiling. "Perfect. Make them ache first."

The women tangled together, licking, fingering, moaning louder and louder, tongues flicking, toys buzzing, thighs glistening with wet. Their cries filled the café, bouncing off the wood panels, drowning the men in sound.

Then, as if rehearsed, they all pulled apart at once.

Four women, flushed and dripping, turned to face the men.

Sophie was the first to speak, her voice shaking but strong. "Out."

The sound of belts and zips was frantic. A dozen cocks sprang into the air, thick, desperate, leaking.

The women smiled wickedly.

Then they pounced.

Maya grabbed one by the tie and yanked him onto the rug, sinking down onto his cock with a scream. Her tits bounced as she rode him hard, hair flying, her cries echoing.

Helen dropped to her knees before two men at once, pumping both cocks furiously, licking one while sucking the other, her tits smeared with precum.

Sophie bent over the table, pulling a man behind her, his cock slamming into her cunt while she screamed for more.

And Alina — silent, unreadable Alina — lay back on a chair, spreading her legs wide, pulling a man's cock into her cunt while another shoved into her mouth. She took both, eyes half-closed, moaning like a sinner at confession.

The room erupted in groans and cries, the air thick with the slap of flesh, the wet suck of mouths, the animal rhythm of fucking.

One by one, the men broke.

Hot cum spurted across tits, faces, tongues. Maya squealed as her cunt was filled, dripping down her thighs as she rode. Helen smeared cum over her chest, licking her fingers clean. Sophie screamed as she came hard around the cock pounding her.

Even Alina cracked, moaning gutturally as both men filled her at once — mouth and cunt overflowing with hot, sticky release. She swallowed greedily, her face shining.

By the end, the floor was wet with sweat and cum, the women sprawled and dripping, the men slumped back in their chairs, ruined.

Amira stepped forward, her voice calm and sharp.

"This," she told the men, gesturing to the four women glistening on the floor, "is the Deep Blend signature. Denial when we want it. Surrender when we choose it. And always… control."

I watched the women, panting, trembling, but radiant. They had passed their test.

Manchester had been claimed.

And this was only the beginning.

✦ ✦ ✦

Chapter 41

The Review

The office felt more like a private club than a workplace — all dark wood, velvet curtains, and leather that smelled of old money. A fire burned low in the grate, the glow reflecting off two crystal flutes of champagne already waiting for us.

The owner rose as we entered. Always immaculate, always composed. But tonight there was something softer in his eyes — satisfaction.

"Victoria. Amira." He gestured to the leather chairs opposite him. "Manchester exceeded every expectation."

We sank into the seats. They felt more like thrones than chairs.

He poured the champagne himself, steady hand, no rush. When he handed me the glass, I felt the weight not just of crystal, but of the recognition behind it.

"To queens," he said.

Our glasses touched lightly, the sound bright against the quiet room.

"You've done more than prove a concept," he said, sitting back. "You've created a signature that men will travel across the country for. Sophie, Maya, Helen, Alina… you turned them into performers in two weeks. That's alchemy. That's Deep Blend."

Amira smirked, crossing her legs. "So what's next, then? Straight to Bristol?"

His smile widened. "Not yet."

He reached into the desk drawer and slid a glossy envelope across the polished wood. First-class tickets. A resort brochure. Details of a private villa, complete with staff, pool, and sea views.

"I don't drive my investments into the ground," he said smoothly. "I keep them polished. Rested. Indulged. You've earned a week of nothing but pleasure. No training, no schedules, no demands. Just you two, fully paid, anywhere you wish. Consider it both a gift and an investment. When you walk into Bristol, I want you radiant, sharp, unstoppable."

I opened the envelope, my pulse quickening at the figures inside — the allowance alone was more than some people made in months.

Amira let out a low laugh. "You're spoiling us."

He shook his head. "I'm preparing you. Queens don't rush from battlefield to battlefield. They arrive in splendor, fully armed. Take the week. Spend it however you please. When you're ready, Bristol will be waiting."

We clinked our glasses again, champagne fizzing against my lips.

Amira leaned back in her chair, smirking. "A week to ourselves, paid to play. He really does know how to keep his queens loyal."

I remembered that proposal email I needed sending to Tyler & Drake but had forgot. 'I must get back to them asap.'

I smiled, the villa brochure warm in my hands. "Then let's enjoy every second of it."

✦ ✦ ✦

Chapter 42

The Holiday

The villa overlooked the sea, white walls gleaming against the blue horizon, the sound of waves crashing below. For the first time in weeks, there were no men waiting in chairs, no trembling cocks to command, no apprentices to guide. Just Amira and me, two queens finally off duty.

And we were starving.

We lay side by side by the pool, champagne sweating in our glasses, the sun on our bare skin. Amira stretched, her bikini falling open just enough to tease me. She smirked, catching my stare.

"You've been watching too," haven't you?" she murmured.

I laughed softly. "Two weeks of nothing but cocks and moans and the smell of sex, and I wasn't allowed a single taste. I'm aching."

Her eyes darkened. "So am I."

The silence that followed was heavy, thick, not the silence of restraint but of inevitability.

I was the first to move. My hand slid onto her thigh, slow, deliberate. She parted her legs instantly, a low growl escaping her lips.

"Finally," she whispered.

We didn't make it inside. We didn't need to.

I pressed her back onto the lounger, tearing her bikini bottom aside, my tongue finding her clit in one desperate stroke. She gasped, her hips jerking, her hand clamping down on my hair.

"God, Victoria…"

Her moans carried into the air, mingling with the sea breeze, the waves, the faint hiss of cicadas. I sucked her harder, lapping up every drop, my own cunt throbbing, dripping onto the lounger beneath me.

She shoved me onto my back, climbing over me, grinding her pussy down onto my mouth, dripping wet. I devoured her greedily, tasting her arousal as she bucked and screamed. Then she slid lower, taking my clit between her lips, sucking furiously until I cried out.

Two weeks of denial exploded in seconds.

We came hard, squirting together, grinding into each other's mouths, the taste of each other's release flooding our tongues.

And then we kept going.

That night, in the cool sheets of the villa, it didn't stop. Fingers, tongues, toys pulled from the cases we'd never bothered to unpack. We pushed each other to the edge again and again, neither of us willing to stop, neither of us willing to let the other win.

It wasn't just release. It was indulgence. A feast after famine.

By morning, the bed was soaked, the air thick with our scent, our bodies aching in the sweetest way.

Amira rolled onto her back, hair tangled, lips swollen, her chest still heaving.

"This," she panted, "was the holiday I needed."

I laughed, exhausted, glowing. "Forget Bristol. I could live here forever."

She smirked, turning to me with wicked eyes. "We've got six days left. Let's see how many times we can ruin each other before then."

And she kissed me again, deep and filthy, already hungry for more.

The villa's privacy was intoxicating, but by the third day we were restless again.

We'd already soaked the sheets, ruined the loungers, filled the tiled bathroom with cries so loud the maid must have known. We had tasted and swallowed and fucked each other raw.

But now? Now we wanted something more dangerous.

We lay side by side by the pool, the late sun spilling gold over the terrace. Other holidaymakers drifted past on the path below, families and couples heading toward the beach. They couldn't see the villa's terrace clearly. But they could if they looked.

Amira caught my eye, her lips curling.

"Shall we?"

I laughed, nerves prickling deliciously under my skin. "You mean… here?"

She slid her bikini bottoms off, tossing them onto the tiles, her cunt glistening in the sun.

"Here."

I dropped between her thighs, my tongue finding her clit instantly, sucking hard, my nails digging into her hips. She gasped, loud, not holding back this time.

Her moans carried into the air — no muffled cushions, no heavy curtains. Just the raw sound of a woman being devoured, echoing down toward the holidaymakers strolling below.

I flicked my tongue faster, wetter, until she cried out. She yanked me up suddenly, flipping me onto my back, straddling my face with her soaked cunt.

"Eat me," she growled, her voice shameless.

And I did, while she bent forward, pulling my bikini top down, sucking my nipples, sliding her fingers inside me until I screamed.

A couple walked past below. I saw them glance up, hesitate, then hurry on with flushed faces.

The thrill sent a jolt through me.

Amira laughed breathlessly, grinding harder against my tongue. "They saw. I know they did. And I don't care."

Neither did I.

I shoved two fingers into her, curling them just right, feeling her tremble, feeling her break. Her juices gushing flooded my mouth as she came, her scream tearing into the open air.

We collapsed against each other, bodies slick with sweat and cum, the sun hot against our bare skin.

Amira kissed me, slow and filthy, tasting herself on my lips.

"We've been surrounded by men for weeks," she panted, "but this — this is just us. Our filth. Our rules."

I laughed against her mouth, already aching for more. "And tomorrow… we'll go further."

Her eyes gleamed wickedly. "Broad daylight. On the beach. Let's see how much they can stand before they run for cover."

And in that moment, I knew — the holiday wasn't just for rest. It was for rebirth. For unleashing every filthy impulse we'd suppressed while playing queens of restraint.

We weren't resting.

We were sharpening our hunger for Bristol.

✦ ✦ ✦

Chapter 43

The Beach Test

The beach was quieter than I expected. Mid-afternoon, the tide low, children gone back to their villas for siestas. Only the occasional sunbather dotted the sand.

That's when we saw him.

A man, alone. Mid-forties, reading under a parasol, sunglasses on, a book open across his lap. No ring. No company. Just him, the sea, and silence.

Amira nudged me with her elbow. "Perfect."

I raised an eyebrow. "You really want to test ourselves here?"

She smirked. "We've been queens for weeks, Victoria. Let's see if the crown still fits."

We laid our towels a little way off but within his line of sight. Not too close. Not too far. Just enough that if he looked up, he couldn't miss us.

I untied my bikini top slowly, stretching my arms above my head as the fabric slipped down, my breasts bare in the sun. Amira lay back, spreading her legs deliberately, the thin triangle of her bikini bottoms tugged to the side just enough to glisten.

I slid down beside her, fingers trailing across her stomach, down, lower. She moaned, loud enough to carry on the sea breeze.

The man's book didn't move. But his head tilted just slightly, sunglasses angled our way.

I pressed my fingers into Amira's cunt, slow and deliberate, while she arched her back, her moans shameless.

"Lick me," she gasped, loud, filthy, deliberate with small squirts of cum released.

I bent between her thighs, tongue flicking her clit, my hair tumbling across her stomach. She cried out, grinding against my mouth, one hand tugging at her own nipples.

The man shifted. The book lifted higher, almost shielding his face. But not quite. His hand disappeared beneath it.

I smirked against Amira's cunt. "He's watching."

She gasped, voice shaking. "Good. Make him break."

We tangled together on the sand, tongues licking, tits bouncing, our moans a performance as shameless as any we'd given in Deep Blend.

Amira slid down my body, sucking my nipple hard, then grinding her cunt against mine, wet against wet, our cries growing louder, filthier.

I stole a glance. The man's chest was heaving. His book trembled. His wrist jerked just slightly, hidden behind the hardback.

"Nearly," I whispered into Amira's mouth.

She laughed breathlessly, then moaned louder, exaggerating every thrust of her hips against mine.

The man shuddered. His shoulders stiffened. The book slipped in his grip. And then it happened — his whole body jolted, a sharp gasp tearing from his throat. His hand froze, his legs tensed, and I knew.

He'd come.

Untouched.

We collapsed against each other, breathless, slick, our bodies shaking with laughter.

"Still got it," Amira panted, grinning wickedly.

I kissed her, tasting her sweat, her arousal. "Still queens."

The man fumbled with his book, pretending nothing had happened, his face flushed even under the shade of his parasol.

But we knew.

We'd made him spill in broad daylight, without laying a finger on him.

And as I lay back on the hot sand, the waves licking at the shore, I realised something delicious: Deep Blend wasn't just a place.

It was **us.**

✦ ✦ ✦

Chapter 44

The Dream Abroad

We were lying on the terrace at sunset, still naked, still sticky from our earlier mischief. A bottle of champagne sat half-empty between us, glasses forgotten.

Amira stretched like a cat, her hair spilling over her shoulders, her smile lazy but dangerous.

"You know what I was thinking?" she murmured.

I smirked. "That you want me to lick you again?"

She laughed, shaking her head. "Always. But no. I was thinking… imagine this place. Right here. A Deep Blend."

I raised an eyebrow. "You mean… abroad?"

"Why not?" she said, propping herself up on her elbow. "We've proven we can train in Manchester. We'll prove it in Bristol. But here? Holiday town, full of wealthy locals, businessmen, bored husbands. And imagine the women we'd bring in — British, like us. Women who crave the sun, the luxury, the thrill. They'd come here for 'a retreat'. And end up performing for men who'd pay through their noses to watch."

I closed my eyes, letting the idea paint itself across my mind.

A villa like this, but larger. Dark wood, velvet drapes, air heavy with heat. Women lounging in lingerie, sipping champagne. Local men, darker, hungrier, desperate to worship at their feet.

Amira's voice softened. "No one here would ever suspect. They'd think it was just another members' club for expats. But inside? Our shows. Our signature. British women, local men. The perfect mix."

My cunt throbbed at the thought.

"You'd have women queuing for it," I said slowly. "The sunshine. The secrecy. The money. And the men… oh, they'd lose themselves for the chance."

Amira grinned. "We could do it. Not tomorrow. Not next year. But one day. Deep Blend Costa del Filth."

I burst out laughing, clutching my stomach. "You are wicked."

She leaned in, kissed me slow and filthy, her tongue tasting of champagne. "And you love it."

I moaned into her mouth, already picturing the scene — two queens sitting on velvet chairs, four new women performing on the tiled floor, local men trembling on the edge, spilling without touch.

"Maybe," I whispered, pulling her onto me, "our empire should go global."

We fucked again that night, but slower, dreamier, both of us caught up in visions of a future where Deep Blend wasn't just in London, Manchester, or Bristol.

It was anywhere we wanted it to be.

And I knew, even as I came again beneath her tongue, that Amira's "what if" wasn't a joke.

It was a plan.

❖ ❖ ❖

Chapter 45

A New Horizon

We came back glowing. Tanned, rested, our bodies sore in the best way possible. For a week we'd drowned ourselves in champagne and each other, but now the villa was behind us and Bristol lay ahead.

Or so we thought.

The owner summoned us the morning after our return. Same office, same champagne glasses waiting, though this time the mood was different. His jaw was tighter, his eyes less certain.

"I won't waste your time," he said, sliding a folder across the desk. "Bristol's off the table. Planning restrictions, licensing, noise objections… the council caved to the pearl-clutches. Too much attention. Too much risk. It's over."

Amira raised a brow. "Just like that? After Manchester?"

He sighed, leaning back. "Sometimes the ground isn't fertile. We move on. London was unique. Manchester worked because of you. Bristol—" he shook his head, "—Bristol's dead."

I felt the champagne go flat on my tongue. Weeks of anticipation gone in a sentence.

But Amira didn't flinch. She leaned forward, eyes sharp, lips curling into that dangerous little smirk I knew meant trouble.

"Then maybe," she purred, "we're planting in the wrong soil."

The owner frowned. "Meaning?"

Amira's gaze didn't waver. "Spain."

Silence.

She let it stretch before continuing. "We've just come back. We saw it with our own eyes. Villas, resorts, expats, locals dripping with cash. Men starving for something discreet, dangerous. And the women? British, restless, hungry. Fly them out under the guise of a retreat. A holiday. But behind closed doors? Deep Blend shows. The signature, the brand — exported."

I felt a shiver race down my spine.

He tapped his fingers against the leather armrest, measuring. "Abroad means risk."

"Abroad means freedom," Amira countered. "No licensing committees. No moral crusaders with clipboards. Privacy, exclusivity, secrecy. And more profit than you can imagine."

The owner's eyes flicked to me. "Victoria?"

I swallowed hard, my pulse quickening. "She's right. We did a test. On the beach. With nothing but a look and a moan. We made a man spill untouched. If we can do that in daylight, imagine what a Spanish villa would become with your name behind it."

His lips twitched — not quite a smile, not quite resistance. But interest.

Amira leaned back, sipping her champagne. "Bristol may be dead. But Spain? Spain could be our kingdom."

For the first time, I saw it in his eyes — the calculation giving way to curiosity. To possibility.

He raised his glass. "Then perhaps we should discuss… Spain."

◆ ◆ ◆

Chapter 46

The Negotiation

We didn't go straight to scouting villas. Not yet. Amira wouldn't allow it — and neither would I.

The owner had power. Money. Reach. But he didn't have our instincts. He didn't understand the women. And without women, Deep Blend was nothing more than a quiet café with expensive chairs.

So we called the meeting. His office again — though this time we didn't sit like guests. We sat like equals.

Amira opened, her tone smooth but sharp. "If Spain is going to happen, there's one rule we won't bend: every woman must know what she's walking into. No false promises. No sugar-coating."

The owner steepled his fingers. "You think they'll come if you tell them the truth?"

I leaned forward, my voice calm but firm. "The truth is the lure. Women aren't fools. They've been lied to enough in life. We won't sell them on 'retreats' or 'getaways'. We'll tell them: 'You'll be watched. You'll be desired. You'll be made to perform'. And the right women? They'll come running."

Amira smirked. "And the wrong women? They'll run away. And good. We don't want them."

The owner studied us, silent, calculating. "That's a risk. Brutal honesty cuts both ways."

I shook my head. "No. It builds trust. The Manchester girls thrived because we showed them what it really was. They weren't tricked. They were transformed. If Spain is to work, the women must arrive knowing exactly what they're agreeing to: the shows, the men, the signature. If they can't stomach it, they don't belong."

Amira drained her champagne in one slow sip. "We're not building a business on lies. We're building an empire on filth. Filth that women choose to revel in. That's our brand."

For a long moment, he said nothing. Then he smiled — a slow, dangerous smile.

"You're right," he said. "That's why you're queens. Not because you perform, but because you know. Very well. Spain will be built on truth. On your signature. On women who come willing, hungry, unapologetic."

He slid a folder toward us — contracts, figures, plans.

"Spain is yours. Show me it can be done."

Amira caught my eye, her smirk mirrored in my own.
We had held our ground. We had set the rules.

And as I signed the page, I realised something thrilling:

We weren't just building Deep Blend anymore.

We were defining it.

✦ ✦ ✦

Chapter 47

The Villa

The car wound through narrow lanes lined with olive groves before the road opened up and we saw it: the villa.

White stone, shutters painted sea-blue, balconies spilling with bougainvillea. A courtyard stretched wide in front, and beyond it — the glimmer of a swimming pool that seemed to spill into the horizon.

I felt my breath catch.

This wasn't just a house. It was a stage.

Inside, the air was cool and still. Terracotta floors, heavy wooden beams, wide rooms begging to be filled with velvet, leather, and laughter. The main hall had double doors opening onto the pool terrace — perfect for transformation into a performance space.

Amira trailed her fingers along a windowsill, her eyes already alight with ideas.

"The café at the core," she murmured. "Typically English, bookshelves, dark wood, the familiar privacy. Members will need that. A place to sit, sip, talk. It has to feel like Deep Blend first."

I nodded, my mind racing. "But here, they can spill outside. Pool loungers. Shaded alcoves. Evenings by candlelight. It doesn't have to be all indoors."

She turned to me, smirking. "And the women can play too. That's the difference. Not a gentleman's club. Not men watching bored dancers. A members' sanctuary. Women teasing each other, women owning the stage, women choosing when to invite the men in."

We walked the grounds, the sun hot on our shoulders. I could already see it.

The pool at night, lanterns floating on the surface, four women laughing as they stripped, slipping into the water while men watched helplessly from the terrace. A shaded pergola where two women lounged in lingerie, stroking each other slowly while daring a man to touch himself. Private alcoves hidden with curtains, not for secrecy but for intimacy.

This wasn't a club. It was an Ecosexation.

A place where desire moved freely, where women could claim space without judgement, where men could ache, spill, and surrender under rules *we* set.

Amira caught my hand, squeezing it hard.

"This is it," she whispered. "This is the next chapter. The villa as the café. The café as the brand. And Spain as our kingdom."

I looked out across the pool, the horizon glittering, and smiled.

"Then let's build it."

✦ ✦ ✦

Chapter 48

Back to the Beginning

It felt strange walking down that street again.

London was grey, the air damp with drizzle, umbrellas jostling for space. So ordinary. And yet tucked behind that familiar dark door was where everything had changed.

The first Deep Blend.

The café where Amira checked IDs like a gatekeeper to another world. Where Daniel sat with his dial flickering red. Where I teased men with the flick of my wrist, the arch of my back, and discovered just how powerful it felt to make them break.

I felt my chest tighten with memory as we pushed through the discreet entrance.

The inside was the same. And different.

The leather still gleamed, the shelves still heavy with books, the soft lamps still casting that warm golden glow. But there was more… confidence. The members moved differently now, not tentative, but tuned to the rhythm of the space. The air carried a quiet electricity, sharper than I remembered.

And behind the counter, clipboard in hand, was a woman I didn't know.

Tall. Dark hair tied neatly back. A calm, assessing look in her eyes as she checked a member's card on a slim tablet.

Amira leaned into me, whispering, "The new Amira."

The thought made me laugh, sharp and soft at once.

When she spotted us, she approached with smooth precision, her voice low, professional.

"Victoria and Amira. I was told to expect you."

Her handshake was firm, her eyes sharp. "My name is Sarah. I manage London now. You left me quite the inheritance."

Amira smirked. "And how's it holding up?"

Sarah's lips curved in the faintest smile. "Better than ever. The members know what this place is for. They respect it. They crave it. And they've heard whispers of Manchester. Even Spain."

The word 'Spain' sent a thrill through me. It was already spreading.

We sat, ordered coffee, and let the room wash over us. That's when I noticed it: the dials.

Still clipped neatly to every table. Still the same soft red and green. But the meaning had shifted.

Sarah explained in her low, calm voice as if she were describing a piece of etiquette:

"Red still means 'do not disturb'. Respect it without question. But green no longer means 'I'm open to talk.' It means: 'I'm ready to play'. Whatever that may mean — a look, a tease, a gesture. As long as it's wanted back."

And as she spoke, I saw it happening.

A woman sat by the bookshelf, green glowing faintly on her table. She crossed her legs slowly, her silk dress slipping back to reveal the dark lace of her stocking tops. The man across from her looked up, flushed, then deliberately tugged his own dial to green. She smiled, just a flicker, and dipped her hand onto her lap..

At another table, two men sat side by side, both dials green. One slid his hand under the table. The other stiffened, then leaned back, eyes half-closed, lips parting. No one interrupted. No one stared. This was simply what green meant now: 'I want, and I'm willing if you are.'

I felt heat curl in my stomach. It was filth, yes, but elegant filth — under rules, under consent, under control.

Sarah returned with our drinks, her eyes scanning the room with quiet authority.

"The members understand. This place is theirs, but only as long as they respect each other. Green never obliges anyone. It only opens a door. The rest…" she let her words hang in the air like smoke, "the rest is whatever they make of it."

I sipped my coffee, strong and rich, my cunt aching just from watching.

Deep Blend London had grown teeth.

And as I looked at Amira, I saw the same gleam in her eyes that I felt burning in mine.

Spain would be ready.

But London had reminded us exactly what we were building.

Sarah left us to our drinks, but I couldn't take my eyes off the room.

Deep Blend was no longer about stolen glances and hidden touches in shadows. It had evolved into something sharper — members testing how far they could go while still keeping the silence intact.

At a corner table, a woman in a pencil skirt leaned forward, her blouse falling open just enough to reveal the edge of a lacy bra. The man across from her tried to keep his composure, but his hand shifted under the table. She caught him. Smiled. Then parted her lips slowly, sliding her fingers along the rim of her glass in a movement that was unmistakable.

His shoulders stiffened. A bead of sweat glistened on his temple. He didn't move his hand away.

Further along, two women sat with books open, dials glowing green. They were angled toward each other but left enough space for the three men at the next table to see everything. One woman slowly lifted her skirt just enough to reveal her bare thigh. The other leaned across, pretending to whisper, but let her hand slip lower — stroking her friend's leg, then higher, and higher, until the men across from them froze in their seats.

The women laughed quietly, not at them, but for them. Every movement was deliberate, choreographed to make their audience ache.

I felt myself getting wet just watching. The room hummed with suppressed moans, with clenched fists under tables, with men biting down on their lips to stop themselves groaning.

And then it happened.

By the window, a woman with red hair pushed her chair back just slightly, then tilted her hips forward. Her green dial glowed. The man she was with swallowed hard, looked around once, and then slid his hand down the front of his trousers.

Not under the table. Not hidden. In plain sight.

His jaw clenched, his body trembling, his cock swelling visibly in his grip.

And she didn't flinch. She watched him, steady, commanding, and slid one slow finger down between her thighs until he groaned, spilling into his hand.

No one intervened. No one gasped. It was simply Deep Blend.

Amira leaned close, her lips brushing my ear.

"Still think we're queens of Spain, Victoria?"

I smiled, heat flooding through me.

"We'll be emperors."

And as the man by the window wiped his hand discreetly, his partner smirking in satisfaction, I knew one thing for certain.

Deep Blend London wasn't just surviving.

It was thriving.

I sipped my coffee slowly, though my body was thrumming.

Watching others was one thing. But sitting idle, silent, as if I hadn't shaped this place with my own hands? That was another.

Amira felt it too. I could see it in the way her fingers tapped her cup, her lips twitching with that dangerous smirk.

Finally she leaned across to me, voice low, eyes gleaming. "Shall we?"

I laughed under my breath. "Let's see how far we can take it."

We shifted our dials to green.

Instantly, three pairs of eyes flicked toward us — men at separate tables, each pretending to read, to sip, to be absorbed in their own worlds. But they weren't. They were watching.

Amira uncrossed her legs, sliding her skirt back just enough to expose the dark silk of her stockings. I leaned closer, my fingers brushing the inside of her thigh as if it were an accident.

She moaned. Soft. Deliberate.

One of the men nearly choked on his drink.

I ran my hand higher, teasing the lace, while Amira tilted her head back, lips parting. Her moan came louder this time, her eyes locked on the man nearest us. His dial flicked from red to green so fast it might have cracked.

I smiled.

I slipped two fingers under the hem of her skirt and entered her wet cunt — not hidden, not apologised for. Her hips jerked. She leaned into me, mouth grazing my ear.

"More."

The man across from us was rigid in his seat, his knuckles white as he gripped the edge of the table. His other hand slid under, trembling.

Sarah appeared at our side. For a moment I thought she'd stop us, but she only crouched slightly, her voice soft, discreet.

"Green is yours to command. As long as you don't break the silence."

Her eyes glimmered with approval. Then she was gone, as if she'd never been there.

Amira smirked, grinding against my hand now, louder, bolder. I licked my lips, let my tongue slide across her neck, and watched the man opposite shudder, his breath ragged, his cock bulging under the table.

It didn't take long.

Her moans grew filthier, mine joining them as I pushed harder, deeper. Across from us, the man couldn't hold back — his shoulders shook, his eyes slammed shut, and with one muffled groan, he unzipped his trousers, pulled out his stiff jerking cock and came right there in the middle of the café.

No one flinched. No one stopped us.

Because this was Deep Blend now.

Amira collapsed against me, laughing quietly, breathless.

"Still allowed to play, then," she whispered, her lips brushing mine.

I smirked, my fingers still glistening, my cunt aching.

"More than allowed," I murmured back. "Expected."

And as we sat there, two queens among their subjects, I realised something delicious:

If this was London, then Spain would be unstoppable.

Chapter 49

The Mansion of Ecosexation

The villa wasn't a café anymore. It wasn't Manchester, or London, or even the private orgy nights we'd orchestrated.

It was bigger. Wilder. Dangerous in its elegance.

It was the mansion.

We arrived at dusk, the air heavy with the scent of jasmine and salt. The pool glowed blue under lantern light, the terrace humming with conversation and quiet laughter. Men lounged with cocktails, shirts open, eyes hungry. Women — British, bold, unapologetic — drifted between them in silk robes, lingerie glinting beneath.

This wasn't random. These women hadn't stumbled in from the bars of Marbella.

Amira and I had handpicked them.

Weeks earlier, before the mansion had even opened its doors, we'd sifted through names and faces. Some found us through whispers of Deep Blend London, others came through contacts in Manchester. We weren't looking for "models" or "professionals."

We wanted women who understood exactly what Deep Blend meant.

No illusions. No soft promises. They knew the rules before they ever set foot in Spain:

- **This is not a job.** It's a choice.
- **You are not for sale.** You are the show.
- **Consent is the crown.** Green only means if you want it too.
- **Your pleasure matters.** More than theirs.

Some women walked away. Most did.

But the few who stayed — those were the ones who belonged here.

We trained them as we had in Manchester — not with tricks or scripts, but with confidence. We showed them how to tease without touching, how to stretch a man's ache until he broke, how to let their own desire fuel the show.

And now, watching them tonight, I knew they had absorbed every lesson.

Two of them stripped by the pool, their laughter ringing out as they slid into the water, silk robes floating on the surface. Men leaned forward in their chairs, dials glinting green at their tables, trembling at the invitation.

Another pair reclined under the pergola, tongues entwined, fingers buried deep, while a man stood frozen just metres away, shaking as he tried not to spill too soon.

Everywhere I looked, sex and luxury fused into one.

This wasn't filth in shadows.

This was filth in daylight, dressed in velvet, crowned with champagne.

Amira leaned into me, her lips brushing my ear.

"This," she whispered, "is the dream we had on the beach. But bigger."

I smiled, watching one of the men groan as a woman whispered something in his ear, his cock visibly straining against his shorts.

"No," I murmured back. "This is better."

Because it wasn't just fantasy anymore.

It was 'Ecosexation.'

And it was ours.

Chapter 50

The Trial by Pool

The pool shimmered like liquid fire under lantern light. Eight men sat in a half-moon along the terrace, drinks trembling in their hands. Shirts loosened, dials green, eyes hungry.

And before them — four women draped in silk robes, each chosen, each trained, each now ready to prove they belonged to Deep Blend Spain.

Their orders were simple.

Make at least one man cum. Without him ever touching himself.

The first to step forward was **Elise**.

Tall, red-haired, lips painted blood-dark. She let her robe fall in one fluid motion, revealing black lace knickers and nothing else. Her breasts swayed as she walked to the pool's edge, her hand sliding down her stomach, slipping into her panties.

She moaned. Long. Shameless. Then pulled her hand free, dripping, and sucked her fingers as though she were starving for her own taste.

One man jolted like he'd been shocked. She turned her eyes to him and smiled wickedly, pushing her slick hand between her breasts and rubbing until her nipples peaked. Her moans turned into filthy little cries, each one stabbing through him.

His body shuddered, his cock bulging hard against his trousers. He gripped the chair so tightly his knuckles whitened, and then—

He gasped. Loud. Messy.

Darkness bloomed across his crotch. His head fell back. Elise smirked, licking her hand clean.

One down.

Next was **Valeria**.

Dark curls, olive skin, a silk robe clinging to her body until she tore it away with a growl. She didn't tease. She demanded.

Dropping to her knees on the tiles, she arched her back and began fucking herself with two fingers, hard and furious, her cries echoing off the stone. "Oh, fuck, yes—fucking harder—" she shouted, writhing like she was possessed.

Her eyes locked on a man at the far left. She grinned through her moans, biting her lip, then spat onto her tits, rubbing the slick across her nipples while panting like a bitch in heat.

The man tried, god he tried, but his hips bucked, his jaw dropped, and he spilled untouched, cock jerking against the fabric of his trousers until it left a wet, shameful patch.

Valeria laughed, spreading her fingers to show the men the gleam of her pussy juice in the lantern light.

Two down.

Lucy and **Isobel** went together.

They were fire and smoke.

Lucy, blonde, pale, delicate-looking, sank onto her knees at the pool's edge, spreading her robe wide. Isobel, raven-haired, curvy, wild, pushed her down flat and buried her face between her thighs.

Lucy screamed. Not soft, not polite — screamed. Her back arched, her tits jiggled, her hands clamped in Isobel's hair as her tongue lapped, slurped, and fucked her open.

Men groaned. Chairs creaked under the strain.

But Isobel wasn't done. She dragged herself up, mouth slick with juice, and crushed her lips against Lucy's, smearing wetness across both their faces. Their tongues fought, loud, obscene, spit dripping onto their breasts.

And then — as if choreographed — they both turned their heads and looked directly at two men on the terrace.

The men broke instantly. One after the other. Bodies jerking, groans spilling from their throats, their trousers ruined with cum.

By the time the four women regrouped, the air stank of sex. Four men sat slumped in their chairs, drained, ruined. The others teetered on the edge, trembling, sweating, begging silently for release.

Amira leaned into me, her smile sharp as glass.

"They've passed," she whispered.

I smirked, heat pooling between my thighs.

"Then give them their reward."

The robes vanished. The terrace erupted.

Elise bent a man over his chair, slamming herself down onto his cock until his groans split the night. Valeria straddled another's face, grinding until he gagged on her dripping wetness. Lucy and Isobel clung to each other as they fucked two men side by side, riding them hard, tongues locked, moans filthy.

The men were undone. The women were radiant. The air was thick with sex.

And Amira and I?

We watched. Queens with champagne in hand. Our girls — our choosing's — proving themselves in the fire.

But watching wasn't enough.

The ache between my thighs was unbearable. The smell, the sounds, the sight of eight men groaning, spilling, breaking under our women's command — it tore the restraint out of me.

I slid my dress up my legs, spreading them wide on the lounger, my fingers diving into my soaked cunt. The first touch made me gasp, loud and raw.

Amira turned to me, smirking, her own hand already buried in her panties.

"Couldn't resist, Victoria?" she whispered.

"Never planned to," I moaned, grinding against my fingers.

We put on our own show.

Two women on the throne, masturbating like royalty, our cries rising to join the chaos at the pool. I rubbed my clit in hard circles, faster, faster, my eyes locked on Elise as she bounced up and down on a cock like she was punishing him.

Amira threw her head back, two fingers buried in her pussy, pumping furiously as she watched Valeria riding a man's face into submission.

Our moans carried across the terrace, spurring them all on. The men looked between the pool and us, their mouths open, their hands gripping thighs, breasts, asses — lost in the frenzy.

I came hard. Screaming, shaking, my body convulsing as my orgasm ripped through me. I squirted over my own hand, wet splattering across the lounger, and didn't care.

Amira followed seconds later, gasping, her body curling tight, her juices soaking her panties. She collapsed against me, laughing breathlessly, her fingers still working slow circles to prolong her release.

We kissed — messy, wet, tongues tangled, sharing the taste of our own lust as the pool roared with cries of men and women climaxing together.

When it finally ebbed, when the men slumped drained
and the women slick and glowing, Amira and I sat back,
smug and sated.

We had chosen well.

Our women had made them cum untouched.

And we had crowned them with our own release.

Spain had its performers.

Spain had its queens.

The mansion was alive.

✦ ✦ ✦

Chapter 51

The Morning After

The villa was quiet the next morning.

No men, no members, no green dials glowing like signals in the dark. Just the hush of the pool water, the scent of jasmine on the breeze, and the low hum of coffee being poured in the kitchen.

Eight of us.

Our four chosen performers. Myself and Amira. And the two locals — the cleaner and the cook, both of whom had stayed the night after watching the chaos unfold, their eyes wide, their lips bitten raw with temptation.

The air still smelt of sex. And it wasn't finished.

It started slowly.

Elise, hair damp from the pool, curled up on a lounger in nothing but her knickers. Valeria came up behind her, pressing kisses down her neck, her hand sliding over Elise's breasts until her nipples stiffened.

Lucy and Isobel sprawled across the cushions, giggling, still sticky from the night before, tracing fingers along each other's thighs.

Amira caught my eye, smirking, and then — to my surprise — the cleaner sat down beside her. Not shy. Not apologetic. Her hand landed boldly on Amira's knee, sliding it higher until Amira gasped.

The cook joined me, lips trembling before she kissed me, hungry, as if she'd been waiting years.

And then there was no stopping it.

Eight women, tangled in heat.

The robes and knickers came off, tossed aside like old skins. Tongues, fingers, moans, cries — the villa shook with it. Elise on her knees licking Valeria's cunt until she screamed. Isobel straddling Lucy's face while Amira coaxed the cleaner into sliding her first ever fingers into another woman.

I lay back, thighs spread, as the cook buried her mouth into my soaking pussy, sloppy and raw, licking like she wanted to drown in my taste. My hips bucked, my moans joining the chorus of others as bodies writhed all around.

We weren't performing.

We weren't teaching.

We weren't proving anything.

We were just women, hungry, aching, devouring each other until the villa itself seemed to sigh with satisfaction.

Eight women. Eight orgasms. And then more. And more.

Until we collapsed in a tangle of sweat, wetness, and laughter, limbs draped across each other, breasts pressed together, mouths swollen, pussies aching but sated.

Amira turned her head against my shoulder, her lips brushing my ear.

"This," she whispered, voice hoarse, "was better than the fuck fest."

I laughed breathlessly, kissing the crown of her head.

"This," I said, "was for us."

And it was.

The first morning of the mansion.

Our Ecosexation had begun.

Chapter 52

The First Ecosexation Night

The air around the villa was electric. Lanterns burned gold, the pool shimmered, and twelve members sat poised — eight men, four women — their dials all glowing green.

Amira and I sat side by side on our thrones, silk dresses already hitched to our thighs, champagne in hand. Tonight wasn't about lessons. It wasn't about training.

Tonight was filth. Pure, unapologetic filth.

The first true Ecosexation night.

Elise

Elise went first.

Tall, pale, hair like flame. She dropped her robe in one smooth motion, stepping down into the pool until the water licked at her thighs.

Her hands slid slowly down her stomach, dipping into her pussy, moaning so loud the men shifted in their seats. She lifted her wet fingers, sucked them, then arched her back so her tits thrust up, nipples already hard.

Her eyes locked onto one man — dark suit, trembling already. She rolled her hips, fucking herself with her hand, moaning, gasping, "Fuck me—oh fuck yes—" louder, filthier, until his jaw dropped.

He tried to fight it, tried to clench his fists, but his body betrayed him. His hips bucked, his cock jerked under his trousers, and with a strangled groan he spilled untouched, cum soaking the fabric.

Elise smiled wickedly, licking her hand clean as he collapsed.

One broken.

Valeria

Valeria was fire — olive skin, dark curls, eyes like knives. She didn't even glance at the men.

She chose a woman.

Pulling her forward, she sat her down on a lounger, spreading her legs wide. The member gasped, shocked, but Valeria pressed a finger to her lips and dropped to her knees.

Her tongue slid along the woman's pussy, slow at first, then harder, filthier, sucking her clit, slapping wet against her folds until the woman cried out. Valeria growled, pushing two fingers deep inside her, fucking her fast, tongue flicking until the woman screamed, legs shaking, juices spilling down Valeria's chin.

The men groaned, their cocks straining, hands trembling at their sides.

The woman came again, sobbing, Valeria's tongue still working until she collapsed against the cushions, ruined and glowing.

Lucy & Isobel

The duet.

Lucy — blonde, delicate, deceptively sweet. Isobel — raven-haired, curvy, wild. Together they were a storm.

They kissed hard, tongues devouring, tits pressing, hands already in each other's pussies. Their moans tangled together, loud, raw, obscene.

Isobel dropped to her knees, sucking Lucy's clit while thrusting three fingers deep inside her. Lucy screamed, pulling Isobel's hair, grinding her cunt against her face until she squirted across her chest.

The men groaned, their cocks jerking helplessly, but still not touching.

Then Isobel climbed onto Lucy's face, riding her tongue, grabbing her own tits, moaning "Fuck me harder—lick my cunt—oh god yes!" until her whole body shook.

A man couldn't hold it. Cum shot across his shirt as he groaned, collapsing back, untouched.

Another followed seconds later, spilling in his trousers, groaning like an animal.

The Break

That was the signal.

The untouched ruins were enough. Now the floodgates opened.

Elise dragged her man into the pool, stripping him bare, riding his cock under the water until the splash and her screams filled the air.

Valeria bent her woman over the lounger, fucking her with a glass toy until she sobbed with pleasure, then shoved it in her ass, making her howl even louder.

Lucy straddled two cocks — one in her pussy, one in her mouth — gagging, drooling, her tits bouncing as she fucked and sucked at once.

Isobel sat on a man's face, riding so hard he choked on her wetness. She slapped his chest, moaning, grinding until she squirted across his chin.

The terrace was chaos.

Men groaned, women screamed. Fingers, tongues, toys, cocks — everywhere, inside everything. Cum spilt over breasts, faces, mouths. Pussies gushed, clits rubbed raw, tits slapped and sucked.

One of the female members climbed onto Elise's lap, grinding her pussy against hers, their juices soaking each other as they kissed sloppily. Another begged for Valeria's tongue while her husband watched, trembling, forbidden to touch until she gave the nod.

Everywhere was raw, relentless fucking.

And Amira and I?

We sat like queens. Our dresses pushed up, fingers buried in our soaked pussies, moaning, gasping, ordering.

"Ride him harder, Elise."
"Finger her ass, Valeria."
"Swallow his cock, Lucy."
"Drown him, Isobel."

We came, we gushed, we squirted watching them obey, our orgasms spilling over our thighs, our cries joining theirs as the night burned on.

By the time it ended, the terrace stank of sex. The pool was cloudy with cum. The loungers stained with wetness.

Twelve members lay ruined, glowing, trembling.

And our women?

Radiant. Slick. Their thighs shaking, their mouths swollen, their pussies dripping, but triumphant.

The first Ecosexation night was complete.

And Spain was ours.

✦ ✦ ✦

Chapter 53

Queens of Ecosexation

The villa was quiet again.

The lanterns had burned out, the pool rippled lazily, and the air smelt faintly of sweat, sex, and jasmine. Our women slept tangled on the loungers, skin glistening with the memory of the night before.

And then he arrived.

The owner. Our benefactor. Our investor.

He didn't need to see the carnage to know. He could smell it. He could feel it. The walls themselves radiated lust, the kind of energy no money alone could buy.

"Victoria. Amira." He kissed our cheeks, poured champagne, and raised his glass. "You've outdone yourselves. Spain is alive. Ecosexation… is real."

The words sank like honey.

He promised rewards — jewels, money, holidays, luxuries. The women, too, were praised and gifted. But what struck deepest was his tone: reverence, as though we weren't just employees. We were Queens.

And then he dropped it.

"Perhaps," he mused, "Ecosexation could travel. France, Italy, perhaps even the States. Imagine the brand—Deep Blend worldwide."

The idea hung heavy in the air.

But he smiled and waved it off. "Not yet. Spain first. One jewel must shine before you cut the next."

When he left, Amira and I sat by the pool, silent.

The choice pressed against us.

We could return to the UK — London, Manchester, the cafés where it all began. Keep the machine humming, play queens of the old halls.

We could stay here — in Spain, at the villa, throned above the pool, queens of Ecosexation itself.

Or… we could walk away. Leave it all. Take the money, the freedom, the memories, and disappear.

I looked at Amira. Her hair was messy, her lips still swollen, her eyes gleaming with power.

"Do we need it?" I asked softly.

She smirked, leaning into me. "Need? No. Want?" She kissed me, slow and filthy, her tongue pressing into my mouth. "Always."

We laughed, the choice unsaid but alive between us.

Queens of Ecosexation. Queens of Deep Blend. Queens of ourselves.

Whatever we chose next — Spain, London, or the wide world — we had already won.

Because we had taken men and women alike, broken them, built them, crowned them with lust.

Because Deep Blend was no longer just a café.

It was a kingdom.

And we were its rulers.

The End

Epilogue

Postcards from a Queen

If you're reading this, it means you've walked every step with me.

From London's hidden corners, to Manchester's experiments, to Spain's villa where Ecosexation was born. You've watched me tease, break, and devour men. You've seen Amira bloom from manager to queen. You've seen us crown new women, tame new cocks, and taste pleasures that even I once thought beyond reach.

And now?

The choice sits in my lap like a lover's hand.

I could return to the UK, play queen of the cafés where this all began. I could stay here in Spain, at the villa, pool shimmering under my rule. Or I could leave it all — money in the bank, lust in my bones, and the memory of every cock, every cunt, every orgasm etched inside me.

Do you want to know what I chose?

Of course you do.

But queens don't always reveal their secrets.

Let's just say this: my glass is still full, my cunt is never empty, and my crown… my crown is still firmly in place.

Deep Blend was never just a café.

It was always a kingdom.

And kingdoms never truly end.

— Victoria